The
Da

*Book 6: Coming Through the Rye*

# The Intimate Memoir
## of
## Dame Jenny Everleigh

## Book 6: Coming Through the Rye

SPHERE BOOKS LIMITED

SPHERE BOOKS LTD

Published by the Penguin Group
27 Wrights Lane, London w8 5tz, England
Viking Penguin Inc., 40 West 23rd Street, New York, New York 10010, USA
Penguin Books Australia Ltd, Ringwood, Victoria, Australia
Penguin Books Canada Ltd, 2801 John Street, Markham, Ontario, Canada l3r 1b4
Penguin Books (NZ) Ltd, 182–190 Wairau Road, Auckland 10, New Zealand

Penguin Books Ltd, Registered Offices: Harmondsworth, Middlesex, England

First published by Sphere Books Ltd 1989

1 3 5 7 9 10 8 6 4 2

Printed and bound in Great Britain by
Richard Clay Ltd, Bungay, Suffolk
Filmset in Monophoto Plantin

Language is like a cracked kettle on which we beat out our tunes for bears to dance to while all the time we long to move the stars to pity.

*Gustave Flaubert* (1821–1880)

# INTRODUCTION

This sixth book of memoirs by Jenny Everleigh contains some extremely interesting comments and descriptions of the social *mores* of the life and times of the leisured classes in the late years of the nineteenth century.

It also features some of the most hilarious and frankly rude writing that appeared in the underground publications of the 1890s. Much of the material appeared in *The Webbed Grotto*, the short-lived successor magazine to *The Oyster* which disappeared without trace around 1894.

Dr David MacSwade, one of the leading experts on Victorian erotica, is of the opinion that the second half of this book – which recalls in telling detail the sexual intimacies during a weekend in the country – was penned by Heather O'Fluffart, one of the fiery 'wild women' who shocked the Victorian establishment by demanding votes for women and other major, radical reforms of Society. Ms O'Fluffart, a close friend of Annie Besant, was known to have dallied with Sir Charles Dilke, a critic of the Royal Family, which may account for the appearance in the narrative of the Prince of Wales. She also enjoyed liaisons with Dr Jonathan Arkley, a well known member of the fast South Hampstead set and another pillar of Society, Sir Graham Giddens, a North East landowner renowned for his many and varied sexual conquests.

As Godfrey Elton-Stanton commented in his preface to Book Four of these diaries (*Jenny Everleigh 4: The Secret Diaries*, Sphere Books, 1988) 'her robust vitality comes across the years through her lusty narrative, especially in Sphere Books' selection which contains some of the frankest yet evocations and descriptions of a variety of sexual acts.'

Certainly, these amusing vignettes give a completely different picture from the usual strait-laced look at life offered by mainstream writers of both past and present.

*Boreham Wood*
*April, 1989*

PART ONE

*21 September 1889*
Readers of my previous diaries [*The Memoirs of Jenny Everleigh 5 – The American Dream*, Sphere Books] will recall that my last entry concerned the insertion into my cunney of the magnificent thick prick of Lieutenant Charles Nicholas of the S S Hyperion, the ocean liner on which I had sailed to and from the New World.

It is now five long weeks since I returned to Albion's sweet shores and quite frankly, dear diary, these have not been the most interesting times which is why I have been somewhat lax in recording events in your pages.

The problem is that quite simply all my friends have been out of town. My old beau Johnny Oaklands has been banished to the country by his Papa until he is satisfied that Johnny is working hard enough to pass his legal examinations. And all my other friends and acquaintances have yet to return to town from the country or from the Grand European Tours that are now so popular. I cannot grumble at this having spent such a fabulous time in America and if there is a better man between the sheets than that randy New York dentist Ronnie Donne I shall be pleased to entertain him. However, since my return to London I have spent my days quietly reading and my nights alone with only cousin Molly's American dildo to keep me company in bed.

With luck, though, this situation will change for the better quite soon as my dear friends the Pokingham sisters, Bella and Beth arrived back in Berkeley Square last week after their summer in Scotland and I have been invited to dine there tonight. Bella has sent round a note earlier today to tell me that their parents will NOT be present as they have been invited to weekend at Doctor Jonathan Arkley's home in the country just west of Barnet. Although she does not mention it, I am sure that like myself, Bella has been fucked by the good doctor and his friend Lionel who seem to have specialized in bedding every lady in London Society between the ages of eighteen and twenty six. [Doctor Arkley and Sir Lionel Trapes were founders of the ultra-fast South Hampstead set who organized wild Society parties in the early 1890s. Arkley treated the Prince of Wales for an unknown complaint in the mid 1890s but was forced to give up medicine after being named in a scandalous divorce action two years later – Editor.]

I have not been told the names of the other guests but Bella has promised an interesting evening and that I should be prepared if possible to bring a change of clothes. Oh-ho, diary, this may mean some recherché after-dinner antics and the way I feel just now, having been denied a good stiff cock for so long (you must pardon my vulgarity), I would even let Connor the butler have his way with me. Actually, I don't think that would be such a bad idea. He is a good-looking man and why should class differences spoil the possibility of a good fuck?

Indeed, I have experienced cocks from all classes and can truthfully report that a man's place in

2

Society has absolutely no bearing whatsoever upon his ability to *faire l'amour*. So I may let Connor fuck me next week if I feel the need as a hard man is always good to find. And I know that the man would love to squeeze my full breasts and kiss my pussey for – I must admit this, diary as no thoughts and deeds are ever censored from your sheets – I have been somewhat naughty as far as our butler is concerned.

I am living all alone in our town house (which is situated in Green Street, Mayfair) as my parents are currently spending a week with my Uncle MacGregor up in Inverness, though I am well attended by our housekeeper Miss Hartfield, Connor and the rest of the staff. Anyhow, the other morning I was partaking of my breakfast dressed only in a blouse and skirt. I had just enjoyed a deliciously warm bath and feeling somewhat hungry I came down without underclothes. I knew that my nipples would be visible as they strained against the thin white cotton of my blouse and I must say that I enjoyed the freedom of not wearing any knickers.

Well, to my delight I could see that Connor was more than a mite flustered by the sight of my titties pressing darkly against the straining almost transparent material – so much so that the poor man dropped the toast-rack and its contents and he was forced to dive down under the table to pick everything up. As his bottom disappeared under the tablecloth I hitched up my skirt and spread my legs wide, giving the lucky butler a close-up of my snatch. He was so surprised that he jerked his head up, banging it sharply against the table. I brought my hand down and rubbed my fingers against my silky pubic hair, trying to keep my upper body still – for Radlett the parlourmaid was still in the room –

3

whilst I attempted to flick my clitty to orgasm.

Alas, Connor's amazement at my brazen behaviour precluded him from active participation though I would have warmly welcomed the feel of his tongue along my moistening slit. However, the poor man was too shocked by what he had seen and perhaps somewhat concussed from the severe blow on the head to be anything except a passive if delighted spectator as I brought myself off as Radlett served me with a nice cup of coffee.

Later that morning I heard voices coming from Connor's bedroom and I tiptoed upstairs and stood by the door which was not fully closed. Now it was my turn to be surprised for what should I see but our butler lying naked on his bed stroking the equally nude body of pretty little Radlett who naturally looked even more desirable displaying her naked charms than in the somewhat severe parlourmaid's black uniform.

'Oh, Amanda,' groaned Connor, 'you just will not believe what happened at breakfast this morning. I still don't think I believe it myself even though I saw it with my own eyes.'

'Johnnie, darling, what are you talking about?' cried his paramour. 'I do hope that the nasty bump on the head you sustained has not affected your senses. If you are unwell, I'll ask Miss Jenny to call for Doctor Abel to have a look at you.'

'There's nothing the matter with me that you cannot cure, Amanda Radlett,' grinned the saucy fellow. 'It isn't Doctor Abel that I need but a prescription of a completely different nature!'

And with those words, the scoundrel pulled Amanda closer to him. I must confess that she was an extremely pretty girl, a fact that I had genuinely

4

not noticed before, full-bodied and yet not run to fat, but firm and curvaceous everywhere, and she presented in her nudity, as luscious a sight of feminine pulchritude as ever I had seen.

Now they kissed and his hand cupped one large breast, I saw that his thick prick was rising stiffly between his thighs and that Amanda had taken the shaft of his truncheon between her long fingers. Her own nipples seemed to grow before my eyes and they stabbed at his palm as he fondled each lovely large bubbie in turn. Then, suddenly rising he placed her down on her back and he knelt between her parted legs. She then pulled his head to her bosom and he turned his lips from side to side, kissing each breast as he encountered its warm, rounded sides and whilst doing so his right arm reached down so that his hand was set between her legs and his fingers played with the thick brush of dark hair that covered her mound.

He parted the rolled lips of her cunney, pale pink they were protruding enchantingly through the nest of black curls and she twisted with desire, rolling her belly silkily on his stiff cock. As he continued to suck hard on those raised up stalky nipples, Amanda threw back her head and moaned with joy. Ever so lightly now, for Connor was obviously a skilled and thoughtful lover who wished his partner to enjoy herself as much as he would, his fingertips traced open the open, wet, slit of her cunt, flicking the erect little clitty that was peeping out. Then the cunney lips were forced apart as he took hold of his own rigid shaft and thrust the red mushroomed knob between the pouting lips of the juicy pussey and Amanda gurgled with delight as he propelled in inch after inch until their pubic hairs were matted together. Connor pulled back slowly and then drove down quickly, pushing the powerful length of his prick full depth inside the lovely girl again and again as she urged him on, closing her feet together at the small of his back to force every last millimetre of that throbbing tool inside her soaking cunt. Such passion brought matters to a swift conclusion and with a cry of 'Here I come!' he jerked up and down in a quite frantic movement before withdrawing his glistening cock for a last final plunge as he spurted his jets of frothy white foam inside her willing womb.

'Oh, that's delicious,' gasped Connor, 'you've milked my prick of every last drop. Oh, Amanda, what a lovely pussey you have!'

'Wow! You really pumped gallons of love-juice into me,' smiled Amanda.

'Y-e-e-s,' said the randy butler. 'But I know you did not achieve the fullest bliss. No, don't attempt to deny it, my dear. I know that you have not yet spent so do let us continue. I will simply polish the silver a little later. Miss Everleigh is an understanding girl, I am sure, and would not want a member of her fair sex to be denied the pleasures of a spend.'

I did not know whether to take this as a compliment or not, but before I could decide I watched Connor's attempt to give the sweet girl her due.

He had now gently placed her on his bed – but sitting with her legs dangling wide apart over the side. He clambered up and then sank down again, gazing at the open cunney that gave full view of the pink inner lips.

'Oh, Amanda, your cunt looks so lovely that I must kiss and suck it and pay my homage to that unique womanly scent,' said Connor, kissing her open cunney with his tongue running the full length of its parted lips. Amanda shuddered as his tongue found her hardened clitty that was sticking out like a

6

miniature cock as he gave it his full attention. Side to side, up and down, she began to jerk wildly. 'Ah, Johnny, Johnny, more more, I'm coming, I'm coming!' she moaned. His hands gripped her hips as she writhed under his tongue's ministrations making it difficult for him to keep his mouth positioned on her clitty. So he took his face away from between her legs and began rubbing and pinching her clitty with his thumb and forefinger. This had the effect of making the girl twist from side to side as her love-juices began to flow and her hands went to her breasts as she played with her own titties, roughly massaging the elongated nips.

'Rub harder, oooh, rub it harder, please, Johnny. Oooh! Ooooh!' she cried as her gyrations increased as she twisted and writhed, heaved and humped until with a shriek she achieved her climax and, imprisoning his hand between her legs she wrapped it tightly between her jerking thighs as she slowly subsided.

Connor stood before her, the red knob of his prick still visible as it stood semi-erect in front of her. Amanda looked mischievously up at his cock and took the twitching pole in her hand.

'Would you like me to suck you off, Johnny?' she enquired somewhat rhetorically.

'Those really are the most unnecessary words you will utter today, Amanda,' smiled my good-looking servant.

And she hopped up on her knees and opening her wide mouth slipped in the luscious knob, enclosing her lips around it as firmly as she could, working on the ultra-sensitive tip with her tongue. She eased her lips, taking in a little more as her hands circled the base of his cock. She worked the loose skin up and

7

down the shaft at the same time as she began to bob her head up and down and his hands now went to the back of her head, pushing her further down on his swollen organ. Somehow she managed to swallow even more of the shaft. Amanda was obviously enjoying herself as she sucked mightily on Connor's thick prick, a sucking that was accompanied by a deliciously erotic squelching noise. She was obviously well-schooled in this activity as well for I saw that Connor could contain himself no longer as he thrust his hips forward and the sperm spurted into her mouth in powerful white streams. She tried as hard as she could to swallow all of his creamy emission but some of the precious fluid dripped from her lips onto the carpet.

The stain will take some explaining away to Mrs Hartfield our housekeeper, I thought to myself, and I almost laughed out loud when Amanda echoed my thoughts.

'Oh, Johnny, look at those spunky stains on the carpet. Mrs Hartfield will be so angry.'

'Don't worry darling,' advised the butler, scratching his balls in a somewhat careless fashion. 'I put a bottle of Doctor Malcolm Campbell's famous elixir under the bed. I have used it for years as a cough mixture, a medicine for the horses and above all as a stain remover and it is most effective in that latter capacity.'

He pulled out a spheroid bottle from under the bed and said: 'Doctor Campbell, despite his Scotch sounding name, hails from Manchester where he makes this marvellous stuff. Only a few chemists in London stock it and I had to walk all the way to Webbs in Wrights Lane to pick up a bottle. Oh my, look at the time. Amanda, don't worry, let's get dressed and I'll see to this stain later. We don't want Miss Everleigh to see us like this!'

Well, I have always possessed a sense of the dramatic and I simply could not resist taking advantage of his words. With a great theatrical sweep, I thrust open the door and I declaimed: 'And what, pray, would you keep from my eyes, sir?'

With a great scream young Amanda Radlett fled from the room leaving the naked Connor to face the music alone. I did not think to call out to her and indeed I dismissed her from my mind. For though she may have imagined that I was angry about what I had just seen, the truth was that the pretty *tableau vivant* I had witnessed merely whetted my appetite to take part in the proceedings as opposed to being a mere spectator.

'Well, sir,' I said with as much severity as I could muster. 'Have you an explanation for this extraordinary behaviour?'

'Oh, Miss Jenny, what can I say? If you dismiss me without a reference I shall finish up in the workhouse. How can I ask you to forget what you have just seen?' pleaded the crestfallen Connor.

'You are asking my forgiveness?' I said.

'I'll do anything you ask,' promised the butler.

'Anything?'

'Anything!'

I pretended to consider the situation with a grave countenance. 'Mmm,' I said after a few moments thought, 'I have a suggestion to make. If you comply with my demand I may well forget about what has happened and we shall consider that the incident never took place – except that if you have had your way with Radlett on the promise of marriage you will not wriggle out of your duty.'

9

'Oh, no, Miss Jenny, I assure you that Radlett has no wish to involve herself with me in such a way. Indeed, she has a fiancé who has plighted his troth and she has accepted his proposal. But he is only a travelling salesman for a publisher of popular novels and you know how badly they are paid. So they will have to wait at least two years before they can save up enough money to be able to begin a life of wedded bliss.'

'She is engaged to be married yet fornicates with you?' I said with genuine surprise.

'Well, yes, Miss Jenny, she does – but only when her fiancé is out of town visiting the provincial booksellers. June has voracious sexual needs and, oh dear, I must admit that I was brought up always to accede to a request from a lady.'

'I am glad to hear of that,' I said, 'as I believe that you will not find my request at all irksome. If you do as I ask, then, as I say, we will forget about this whole affair.'

'Oh, Miss Jenny, you are the epitome of kindness,' gasped the relieved Connor. 'Now how may I be of service?'

I closed the door of the room gently behind me and locked the door.

'Your task is very simple,' I said softly, unbuttoning my blouse. 'I want you, as the colloquialism has it, to fuck the arse off me!'

Well, of course the poor chap was absolutely stunned as these words tumbled out of my mouth! He looked on open mouthed as I shrugged off my blouse and folded it neatly over an adjacent chair. I sat down on the bed and took off my shoes.

'Do I have to undress myself or will you help me?' I asked.

Connor could hardly believe his eyes but I must say that his cock was the first part of his body to grasp the fact that I was truly in earnest. As I pulled down my skirt his thick prick rose majestically upwards. It really was a magnificent tool, at least seven inches long and smooth to the touch. He accepted my invitation to pull off the rest of my clothing and in a trice I was lying there, fully nude and yearning for him to relieve my unrestrained lust.

I had always thought that the lower classes possessed only imperfect knowledge of the joys of *l'amour* but Connor proved to be an exception to the rule and proved himself to be an excellent lover.

He first knelt between my open legs and deftly parted my soaked cunney lips with his fingers. I shuddered as he smoothly massaged the insides of my cunney lips with his tongue, an arousing prelude rarely practised, alas, in Britain although our Continental friends are skilled at this art. He moved from my inner lips to my clitty and began to suck on it very lightly while his hands moved quickly up to my distended nipples and rubbed them in small, precise, circles which I always find produces a quite delicious sensation. Already I was floating by now, my orgasm building up inside me.

Just as my pussey began to pulsate he slipped his tongue deep into me and began to tongue-fuck me while one hand squeezed my nipple and the other moved down to massage my clitty. I stifled a moan as the exquisite pleasure of a tremendous spend surged through me.

Without missing a beat he moved his body up over mine, pulling my legs onto his shoulders and sliding that huge cock deep inside my womb. He buried himself inside me with a deep, strong thrust that mashed my clitty against his pubic bone and made me spend even more. He held us together very still, smiling as my spasms stopped and I lay there gasping for breath. Now he began to stroke his prick in and out, penetrating with lightning force and speed. He managed to keep this up for maybe a full minute and I would be delirious with pleasure as I spent. Then he stopped and just held still until the orgasm ceased. He did it over and over again until I could barely breathe and perspiration rolled down our bodies. Then with one almighty thrust he groaned and I felt his body stiffen. A second later, my pussey was flooded with a boiling ocean of his spunk and I cried out in ecstasy as my raw nerves finally found relief.

He lay on top of me, careful to keep his cock deep inside my cunney and we held each other quietly as we calmed and our hearts slowed. 'Have I earned your forgiveness?' quipped the randy butler.

I nodded my assent and murmured: 'Connor, you fuck like a rattlesnake, as they say in Arizona, and I assure you that this verdict is not given out lightly. If you carry out the rest of your duties in such an exemplary fashion I am sure that you will continue in our service at least until your cock drops off!'

'Thank you, Miss Jenny,' he said delightedly. 'And may I tell Radlett that she too is forgiven?'

'Certainly, you may,' I said graciously. 'However, next time you fuck her, do be careful to lock the door.'

'I most certainly will,' he promised, assisting me to my feet. 'And now, how else may I be of service to you?'

'Run me a bath,' I said. 'I am going out for a short walk and will only require light meals today and tomorrow for luncheon for tomorrow I am dining at the Pokinghams in Berkeley Square. Incidentally, tell Graeme the coachman that I shall leave at eight o'clock and I will send a message out when I will want to return. I may well decide to stay the night at the Pokinghams so if I have not returned by one o'clock in the morning, you may lock up and retire – to whatever bed you wish, but as I said, do remember to ensure your privacy.'

We pulled on our clothes and after my bath I did indeed enjoy a short constitutional in Hyde Park. After luncheon, the journalist Freddie Newman came round with a book he had borrowed from our library. It was wrapped and sealed in thick brown paper which excited my curiosity – but I am busy now writing this narrative into my diary and I will open the parcel at a later time. Oh, I do hope that I shall not be disappointed by the Pokingham sisters' party tomorrow. I have been so bored the last few days that I am looking forward to this diversion with mounting excitement – especially if there will be some real mounting after we have dined!'

*23 September 1889*

Well, dear diary, as you know I enjoyed a most splendid evening at the Pokinghams – indeed I cannot recall a more enjoyable evening except perhaps when Johnny Oaklands and Harold Le Meshigunah entertained me at the Jim Jam Club last year. [See *The Intimate Memoir of Dame Jenny Everleigh, Book 4: The Secret Diaries*, Sphere Books, 1988 – Editor.]

What a swell party, as the Americans would say – you must forgive me diary for the occasional use of the American vernacular but I have just returned, as you well know, from six weeks glorious holiday in the United States where in the company of my madcap cousin Molly Farquahar (was ever a girl aptly named!) I enjoyed many days and nights of fucking and sucking such as I have never experienced before. [*See The Intimate Memoir of Dame Jenny Everleigh, Book 5: The American Dream*, Sphere Books, 1988.]

Let me first jot down the guest list for the Pokingham dinner. Bella and Beth Pokingham are slightly older than I, Bella being the older girl is, I believe twenty three or perhaps twenty four years of age whilst Beth is just twenty one. Both girls are strikingly attractive and Beth especially is of singular beauty. She is tall, almost five feet ten inches in height with a willowy figure and a pert pretty face with bright brown eyes which match her long, exquisitely soft hair that falls down in ringlets almost to her shoulders. Although my legs are by no means short and stumpy, I must confess that they cannot rival Beth's in length and my boy friend Johnny Oaklands once remarked that Beth's legs look as though they go up to her armpits! This made me jealously wonder how he knew such intimate information but he assured me that his remark was pure conjecture.

Bella is shorter than her sister and also possesses a pretty face and though until last night I had never seen them in their naked beauty, always looked amply endowed in both breasts and buttocks. Her nose is a mite long and again, and at Lord Bucknell's Spring Ball, I heard Johnny Oaklands comment 'like nose, like clitty!' and always wondered whether the old country saying had any grain of truth in it – well, last night I found out!

The sisters were squired by Doctor Roy Stevenson, the well-known Society specialist in intimate affairs who escorted the gorgeous Beth, and by Captain Jock Gibson of the Third Edinburgh Cavalry Regiment. Doctor Stevenson has been known to our family for some years although I have always been a mite suspicious of this silver haired Romeo whose twinkling blue eyes and jolly repartee have captured the hearts – and other parts! – of many beautiful ladies in the highest echelons of Society. My dear friend Lizzie Thompson always wondered why she was asked to remove her blouse and undergarments when she consulted Doctor Stevenson about a pain in her left ear.

The dashing Captain Gibson was new to the London season though he was known to have enjoyed many conquests up in his own fair city. He too was a most agreeable conversationalist as indeed was the partner the sweet sisters had chosen for me. Count Johann Gewirtz, a dashing, most handsome young

15

man who, fortunately as far as I was concerned, spoke English and French quite effortlessly. Why cannot the English learn languages as easily as our Continental cousins, diary? Most of us leave school with only barely adequate French plus perhaps a smattering of Latin. However, I digress and will complete the listing of the dramatis personnae. The other couple making up our octet were Helene Sylvan, the petite ballerina and Morris Cohn-Bickler, the wealthy scion of the well-known banking dynasty.

Let us begin at the beginning (a very good place to start); my coachman, Graeme deposited me at the Pokinghams at eight fifteen promptly and the company was all assembled by half past the hour. At first, our small talk was of a general tone about the weather, our friends and all the general tittle tattle that exercises the inhabitants of Mayfair.

Count Gewirtz and Morris Cohn-Bickler were engaged in a deep discussion about where Count Gewirtz should purchase a town house in London.

'Do you need to stay in London often, Count?' asked Mr Cohn-Bickler.

'Not as often as I should like,' said my escort in his pleasant slightly accented voice, 'for I do declare that despite the claims of Vienna and Paris, in my opinion the prettiest girls are to be found in London.'

I blushed demurely and smiled my approval though I stayed silent at this stage.

'Well, if you do need your own place here, I would recommend St John's Wood as an area to buy or to build,' declared the banker.

'I don't know the area very well,' said the Count. 'Am I right in thinking that you are talking of the district just north of Regent's Park?'

'Absolutely right,' said Mr Cohn-Bickler, 'and I

would think that this is just the right place for you. There are handsome houses and elegant Regency villas galore along with some modern erections.'

'There is no wood any more, though, is there?' I asked.

'No, no, no although it was once a royal woodland. It was named after the Priors of St John who lost their land during the Reformation but the tranquillity has been somewhat disturbed in modern times.

'Many people of note live there to benefit from its clean air and picturesque surroundings. Perhaps that is why so many artists and writers have chosen to live there. Now I know you are a connoisseur of art, Count, for Sir Michael Segal has told me that you possess two Rembrandts and a Van Gogh in your collection,' said Mr Cohn-Bickler.

'Ah, you must not believe all that you are told, Morris,' smiled my handsome partner.

'I never do, Count, and I doubt if Miss Everleigh does either.'

The two men both turned to me as I said carefully: 'It depends who I am talking with, gentlemen. I am sure in company such as this I can believe every word I hear!'

'Don't be too sure, Miss Everleigh –'

'Oh, Jenny, please, Count.'

'Very well, Jenny, and you must call me Johann, or Johnny if you prefer the anglicized version of my name.'

'And do call me Morris,' said Mr Cohn-Bickler, so a pleasant informality was established between us and between Helene Sylvan, Morris's dining partner who had ambled across the room to join us.

Helene was a most amiable girl and although famous for her many roles on the stage all over the world she was very pleasant and easy to talk with and did not 'put on the style' as so many performers on the stage are prone to do in company.

'Helene, I have not seen you since, my goodness, it must be last November in New York,' said Count Gewirtz.

'I do believe you are right, Johnny,' smiled Helene, 'and thank you again for the charming compliments and lovely bouquet of flowers you sent round back-stage.'

'Not at all, not at all, Helene, but more importantly I understand that you will shortly be starring in a new ballet at the Alhambra next month. Alas, I may have to visit my estates in Galicia just then so I doubt if I will be able to see you dance much before Christmas.'

'Is Signor Cascara still managing director at the Alhambra?' Morris enquired.

'Oh, yes,' replied Helene. 'Signor Cascara and Madame Moser still produce the latest terpsichorean wonders there.'

'I love the musical theatre,' said Morris, 'and I am not ashamed to say that I obtain a real thrill every time I visit the Alhambra which is the very head-quarters of dazzle and glitter, leg and limelight.'

'You will enjoy our new production, "Estelle du Quentonne,"' said Helene, 'as not only is the story line full of drama, love and passion. The production is particularly lavish and you will marvel at the gorgeousness of the scenery and costume – though in your case, Johnny Gewirtz, your attention will doubt-less be focused more on the silk-stockinged legs of the corps de ballet!'

'I cannot deny it,' laughed the Count, 'but more especially so when you will be on stage, Helene my sweet.'

We chatted on in gay fashion until Aspiso, the Pokinghams' old but discreet Italian retainer, announced that dinner was served and we trooped into the Pokinghams' magnificent *salle à manger* to partake of our repast.

The repast was lavish and the wines quite munificent in both quality and quantity so by the time the ladies were about to retire I was feeling totally replete.

I was about to rise when Bella Pokingham – who already enjoyed a reputation as a radical – piped up: 'I don't see why we should be excluded from the table just so the men can enjoy brandy and cigars and tell risqué stories. I have no desire to smoke cigars myself (nor cigarettes come to that as I believe smoking to be a vile habit) but why should we women be cast aside like second class citizens at the end of a dinner party?'

'Well, I suppose the custom allows us to retire gracefully to the powder room,' ventured Helene Sylvan.

'True, but the men can relieve themselves simply by excusing themselves from the table between courses especially after the main course,' rejoined Bella, 'I think it unfair, don't you agree, Jenny?'

To be frank, the idea of retiring to leave the men to their own devices for a time has always irritated me somewhat and I took Bella's side in the discussion. As for the men, Captain Gibson and Morris Cohn-Bickler plumped for the status quo but Doctor Stevenson and Count Gewirtz took the progressive view as espoused by Bella and myself.

'I believe you and I are in the minority, Morris,' laughed Captain Gibson, 'so as we are now in a democratic age, I suppose we must surrender gracefully.'

'Up to you, Cap'n,' said Morris somewhat indistinctly as he polished off his glass of champagne, 'I don't really care a flying fuck either way, if the ladies will excuse my language.'

'An interesting observation,' said Johnny Gewirtz, 'for to the best of my knowledge, none of the brave balloonists have ever even asked females to take a voyage in the sky let alone enjoy their favours whilst in the air.'

'It would be fun to fuck whilst flying,' said Beth Pokingham.

'A sucking off in the sky perhaps?' asked Captain Gibson. 'Or, if not, how about in Berkeley Square in the comfort of your bedroom, darling Beth?' he added hopefully.

'You may not be disappointed but don't be impatient,' said Beth with a twinkle in her eye.

Anyway, it was finally and unanimously decided to be unconventional and we ladies stayed in the dining room whilst the brandy and cigars were brought round by Aspiso and his underlings. Fortunately, only Morris Cohn-Bickler and Captain Gibson chose to smoke (readers of my previous diaries will recall that like many girls, I detest the smell of tobacco which lingers on the breath as well as polluting the air) but all the diners, both male and female, partook of the fine cognac and other liqueurs offered by Aspiso.

'Well,' said Bella with a mischievous twinkle in her eye, 'I am waiting for the wit and wisdom, gentlemen. Surely, the presence of the ladies does not inhibit you from speaking freely.'

'Certainly not,' laughed Count Gewirtz. 'Why, Captain Gibson told me earlier this evening of a quite extraordinary happening in Edinburgh last Thursday night. Come now, Jock, you won't be shy to tell the story in front of the girls?'

'Och, I'm nae sure,' demurred the gallant Captain, winking at me across the table. 'I'm sure that I have no desire to cause offence. The anecdote concerns matters of, ah, an intimate nature and –'

'Oh, come on, Jock, stop fartassing about!' snapped Beth. 'You know full well that round this table we all call a spade a spade.'

'Or even a fucking shovel!' added Bella and the company dissolved into hilarious laughter.

'Oh, very well then,' said Jock Gibson with a good-natured smile, 'as you all want to hear about what happened to me I had better tell you.

'I was taking my daily constitutional after luncheon – whenever possible I always walk along Princes Street which I am sure you will agree is one of the most admirable streets in Europe. I noticed a pretty young girl, smartly attired, selling copies of a magazine on the pavement outside a coffee house. She seemed to be a lady as opposed to the usual street urchin selling papers on the street so I walked up to her and looked at the magazine she was waving in her hand.

'She turned to me and we recognized each other – she was young Mary, the sister of my old friend Sir Leon Oxford, the Laird of Maccuck who studied with me whilst we were at Edinburgh University.

'"Why, Mary," I said with some surprise, "What on earth are you doing here?"

'"Hello, Jock," she answered, "Would you like to buy a magazine from me? It's the latest edition of *The Emancipator*, the journal of the Scottish Branch of The Women's Suffrage Movement."

'"I'm not hugely interested in the subject," I

replied, "although I readily concede the case of votes for women."

'Her eyes sparkled with delight – "Oh, Jock, you wee darling," she cried, "if only there were more enlightened men of influence like you. I must tell you that I've always admired you and now that you tell me that you are a convert to our cause, I'd, well, yes, why not I'll tell you, I'd like to give you a great big kiss!"

'"Don't let me stop you," I replied, eyeing the pretty girl up and down. "Well, not here, Jock," she murmured, putting down her stack of magazines. "Once I sell these magazines, we could retire to the privacy of my apartments over the road."

'"No need to wait any longer," I said briskly, "here, I'll give you a sovereign for the lot, and your work will be over."

'"Oh, Jock, you are kindness personified," she said with gratitude. "We could leave the magazines here and people can take them gratis."

'I gave Mary the sovereign and we arranged the magazines in a neat pile with a card saying "Take a free copy" on the top and we crossed the road to her apartments. Once inside we took off our coats and Mary said 'Can I offer you a drink, Jock? My maid is out this afternoon but I can pour a whisky well enough."

'"Thank you, Mary but not right now," I answered, "though I will take up your offer of a kiss!"'

Captain Gibson paused to sip some iced water from one of the exquisite little silver goblets Count Gewirtz had given the Pokinghams as a housewarming gift when the family moved into the imposing country house built for them by the talented young architect Phil Bosinney in 1886.

22

He continued: 'To my astonishment and un-qualified delight Mary took me at my word and almost leaped into my waiting arms. She brought up her pretty face next to mine and our lips glued together as we welded our bodies together in a passionate embrace.

'Our tongues explored each others' mouths as we sank back onto the couch. She then freed her lips from mine and, leaning over, began to unbutton my trousers and took out my naked cock which was, as you may well imagine, standing up to its full height. Tickling it lightly, she pulled down the foreskin before wrapping her rich, red lips around the strain-ing shaft to suck lovingly at it until I was in the seventh heaven of ecstacy.

'The dear girl could see that her sweet ministrations would make me spend my seed too quickly so she stopped sucking and with a light kiss of farewell on the top of my knob, she lay back to let me pleasure her body. We kissed again and I ran my hand under her dress up her thigh and immediately found out that the naughty minx was not wearing any knickers! My trembling hand parted her legs and felt for her moist pussey. I slipped off the couch and kneeling in devoted homage, I buried my head between her legs as she opened them wider in a welcoming gesture. My tongue worked around her clitty and her hands on my head forced my tongue deeper into her soaking wet cunt. Och, my prick fairly ached to be inside her as her warm love-juices trickled down my throat.

'"May I fuck you now, Mary?" I humbly asked the pretty maid.

'"Of course you may, my darling Jock," she replied with a smile, "I would like nothing better in the whole wide world!"

'Without further ado I slipped off the rest of her clothes and stripped off my shirt, trousers and underclothes – I am sure that all members of this company will agree that unless extreme cold precludes it, a naked fuck is far more exciting than a coupling with your clothes on – and Mary lay on her back, her legs spread wide with her hand on my cock, pulling me to her. She inserted my knob directly into her sopping pussey and as it slipped in I sucked on her erect little nipples, moving my head from one to the other until she was in a very frenzy of excitement. I fucked her quite powerfully, plunging my prick in and out of her pussey, my balls banging against her bottom as my shaft slid in until our pubic hairs mashed together.

'She squealed with delight as she reached orgasm and just moments later I felt my climax approaching. I gasped as the boiling juices came jetting out of my cock, flooding her cunney with white froth as we writhed together in paroxyms of pleasure until, like runners after the white tape has been breached, we gently slowed down to a standstill.'

There was silence for a few moments until Bella Pokingham murmured: 'Goodness me, Jock, it certainly sounds as if you thoroughly enjoyed yourselves.'

'That we did, Bella,' agreed Captain Gibson, 'and without wishing to brag, I suppose I should add that Mary had the grace to thank me for a lovely fuck and I assured her that I should be the one to first express my thanks.

'"We must do this again, Jock," said Mary.

'"Aye, my dear, but not right now." I replied.

'"Oh, Jock, I am sure that I could suck your lovely prick up to a full erection," said Mary.

'"I'm sure you could," I said, "and I would be

delighted to let you do it, but I think I can hear footsteps outside."

'"Oh, damn!" said Mary. "It must be my brother Leon who said he might be calling about this time."

'We looked at each other's naked bodies for a second or two and then – well, I am certain that we must have broken every record in the book for speediness of dressing! Fortunately, Leon did not possess the keys of the apartment and we did not keep him waiting for too long a time after he rang the front doorbell.'

'A splendid tale, Jock,' said Dr Stevenson, 'although what a shame that Leon Oxford did not delay his visit by an hour or so. For I am sure you would both have wished to continue the joust.'

'Well, at least they managed to finish what they had started, Roy,' said Beth, 'and as the author of the most famous book in the world on fucking, I'm sure you will tell us that this is most important of all.'

'Yes, of course,' said the good doctor, 'I am of the opinion that once the senses have been aroused we should, ah, travel to our termini, so to speak though there are many ways to take our journeys and there are no set times or routes to which we must adhere.'

'It must be awfully frustrating to be interrupted in the middle of making love,' said Count Gewirtz, 'I am sure that only an earthquake would prevent me interrupting a session of *l'amour* half way through the proceedings.'

'Don't say that, Johnny,' said Morris Cohn-Bickler gloomily, 'Unfortunately I have been in a position where proceedings had to be postponed – or in this case, cancelled!'

'How awfully tiresome, Morris,' I said sympathetically, 'would you care to tell us about it?'

'Oh, I have no wish to bore the company with a tedious tale,' said Morris, a smile playing about his mouth.

'Come on, come on,' we chorused, 'let's hear all about it.'

'Well, if you insist,' he began, 'but first, Jenny, perhaps you would kindly pass me the port.'

I complied with his request and Morris began his story.

'My tale begins at the house of my old friend Sir Lionel Trapes,' Morris began, 'a gentleman known to some of you, perhaps, as the most noted collector of gallant literature in London.

'Lionel is an old friend of mine, since we were at University together not far from here at the new London School of Economics and Political Science. Not that Lionel has to work, of course as his family are wealthy landowners in Kent but he studied political economy and for some years now he has worked in some high administrative capacity in the Home Office. I mention these facts as they are germane to my story.

'Anyhow, one day last year I called at his town house in St John's Wood as he had written to me asking my advice about some personal financial affairs. It was a particularly warm day for April – perhaps you will all recall how pleasant a month it was this year – and I arrived punctually at half past three in the afternoon. To my surprise, the door was opened not by Dunn, his old butler nor even Bradstreet his faithful footman but by a pretty, no exquisitely beautiful, young girl dressed in a black maid's uniform with a sparkling white apron – an outfit that set off to perfection her pert mass of blonde hair, large cornflower-blue eyes, a tiny nose and pearly white rows of teeth that shone in the sunlight that poured down onto the doorstep.

'"Good afternoon, sir. Are you Mister Morris Cohn-Bickler?" said this adorable apparition with a shy little giggle.

'"Indeed I am," I replied, unable to tear away my gaze from her lovely face.

'"I am Penny, sir," she said, opening the door for me, "and I have a message for you from Sir Lionel." And after taking my hat and coat she slipped a note from my old friend into my hand. It read as follows:

'Dear Morris,

My sincere apologies but I have been called to a meeting with the Home Secretary – I shan't be back till about half past four. Meanwhile, I'm afraid that Dunn and Bradstreet have the afternoon off but young Penny will entertain you in any way you fancy – and I mean any way, my dear chap.

If you are game, just whisper to Penny that you would like to be entertained in the same manner that she entertained Doctor Arkley last week!!! Of course, if you prefer, you can simply tell her that you will return later this afternoon or call me tonight to fix another time for our discussion. But I doubt if you will do this, Morris, unless you are extremely fatigued in mind and body!

Sincerely,
Lionel

'Lionel was absolutely correct in his assumption!! I whispered hoarsely to this lovely lass that I wished to stay as Sir Lionel had been detained and that I would not be averse to being entertained in the same fashion as she had entertained young Doctor Arkley – who by coincidence is my own physician!

27

'"Ah, I am glad," she said and took hold of my hand, "do come this way into the guest room." We went upstairs and Penny held open the green door of the *salle privée*. She followed me in and softly closed the door behind us, locking it and throwing the key down on the rich, thickly piled carpet. I could hardly believe my good fortune as I took her hands in mine and cast my eyes down to her swelling bosoms which were covered by the black material that was drawn tightly over her full breasts.

'She smiled at me, and then suddenly, as if remembering what she had to do, set to work unhooking her dress and loosening the strings and laces. In a trice she was naked and her bosom, now quite bare, was rising and the swell of those firm young breasts generated a powerful excitement throughout my frame. Her breasts were well separated, each looking a little away from the other and tapering in lovely curves until they came to two rich crimson points. These taut nipples acted as magical magnets so that I desperately desired to squeeze those succulent globes.

'What a truly magnificent pair of bubbies she possessed! I felt her pouting, hard nipples against my fingers as my cock began to rise from its torpor into an erection. Then the darling girl kissed me and in an instant her tongue was filling my mouth, probing, rousing and caressing until my cock was as stiff as a guardsman at attention, throbbing rhythmically in expectation of the delights to come.

'Penny slid her hands to the front of my trousers and quickly unbuttoned my fly as I wrenched off my belt. She quickly pulled down my drawers and grasped my hot prick with both hands, rubbing up and down the shaft with such delicacy that almost immediately I found myself climaxing with the white froth gushing out of the purple dome in a swift miniature fountain as a shuddering orgasm of pleasure rammed through my whole body.

' "Oh, dear me," she murmured. "We cannot stop the entertainment so soon." '

' "I've started so I'll finish," I replied, "as I am sure that I can come to scratch with a little help from a friend." '

'Well, before I knew what was happening –'

'She presented her bill for services rendered!' interrupted Count Gewirtz.

'Who's telling this story, Johnny, you or me?' retorted Morris.

'Shush, Johnny, this is a very interesting vignette' said Beth Pokingham, 'if you promise not to interrupt I'll suck your cock after coffee.'

'I think I'm entitled to first go at the Gewirtz member,' I said, emboldened by my second cognac, 'after all, he did escort me and not you into dinner.'

'Quite right, Jenny,' laughed the gay Count, 'but so as not to cause any bad feeling you may suck it together. First though, let us hear out Morris's story.'

'Thank you very much,' said Morris heavily. 'Anyhow, almost before I knew what was happening there I was stark naked sitting on a large leather chair and Penny was gently stroking my cock with her skilful long fingers. Soon my weapon had regained all its former stiffness and suddenly her tousled blonde hair was between my legs as she kissed my now rampant prick. Her tongue flicked out and teased the mushroom dome and then she opened her lips wide and encircled the knob as instinctively I moved my lower body upwards to push my yearning cock even further into her mouth.

'Not even Lady F-----r, renowned throughout Europe for her cocksucking, could match the abilities in the fine art of this pretty parlourmaid.

'Her marvellous tongue washed all around my knob, savouring the juices and her teeth scraped the tender flesh around the rim as she drew me in fully between those luscious lips, sucking slowly from the top all the way down to the base and then from base to top, delighting me to new almost unbelievable heights of pleasure.

'How beautifully she sucked my cock, taking my shaft between her teeth and cheek that sent me into a frenzy of joy. To ensure that I did not spend too quickly, each time I felt my balls hardening she eased up – even without my telling her – to prolong the action.

'Finally, she climbed on top of me with her knees on either side. She pulled open her cunney lips with her fingers and began to rub her pussey across the end of my cock. Then she guided my straining shaft into her pussey, slowly tightening the walls of her cunt so that she held me in place. Many girls are unsure as to how to ride a vertical cock, St George style, but Penny rode me with great assurance, twisting her hips and bumping and grinding away, my cock jammed inside her sopping pussey. I grasped hold of her writhing body and pulled her down so that her titties were against my lips. When I began to nibble on her cherry-coloured nipples she started going truly wild, thrashing about like a girl demented as she began to climax, rocking backwards and forwards as I too pushed hard and felt the frothy white spunk shoot out of my cock, mingling with her own passion juices. "Aaaaah! Aaaaah! More, more!" she shouted as the final flood of hot, creamy sperm flooded into her and I felt her shudder as she drained me of every last drop of spunk as I pumped out my fluids into her dark, secret warmth.

'We lay there for a while, panting with exhaustion. I had been expecting a dull financial meeting with Sir Lionel Trapes but instead here I was lying next to a beautiful nude girl having just made passionate love to her. Or if the truth be told, having just had her make love to me!

'"Would you mind kissing my pussey, sir?" said the delightful creature, "for I do believe that I could spend again!" Would I indeed? Such a silly question to ask. Without further ado I caressed the inside of her thighs, marvelling at their soft texture. Her legs trembled as I knelt down between them, smelling the sweet scent of pussey that wafted up to my nose. I parted the silky strands of her blonde muff with my fingertips to reveal her still swollen clitty and as I worked my face into the cleft between her thighs I could not help but notice how clean and appealing her pussey looked.

'By this time I had one hand under her derrière for elevation and with the other I spread her cunney lips with my thumb and middle finger. I placed my lips over her clitty and sucked it into my mouth where the tip of my tongue began to explore it from all directions. As I lapped at her pussey I could feel her clitty expanding as her legs twitched up and down as she drummed her heels onto the carpet.

'I found the little button under the fold at the base of the clitty and began to twirl my tongue around it – just as you recommend in you book, Doctor Stevenson – and as I moved it up and down very rapidly, Penny became even more excited. The faster I vibrated my tongue, the more reaction I achieved from the lovely girl.

'She began to moan loudly and I could taste the juices flowing out of her. She was delicious and I was tempted to suck away even harder. Pushing my mouth hard up against her cunney I began to move my entire head back and fourth until her pussey was dripping wet as my tongue moved even more quickly along the silken grooves of her cunt, licking and lapping her juices that ran like a stream down her thighs, mixed of course with my own saliva. With each stroke she arched her body in ecstacy, pressing her erect little clitty up against my flickering tongue.

'"OOOOOH! OOOOOOOH!" she moaned and then let out a little scream of joy as I felt her explode as her clitty moved violently up and down against my mouth.'

'But what has all this, interesting story though it be, to do with being interrupted?' enquired Captain Gibson.

'Ah, I'm just coming to that matter,' said Morris Cohn-Bickler, 'for remember now that Penny and I had enjoyed a truly memorable bout of fucking and when engaged in this activity time just passes by.

'Anyways, there we were, entwined together with my hand idly passing over her swelling naked bosoms when Penny said: "You know, sir, I have a fancy for something unusual. Mrs Whitehouse, the cook, makes delicious ice-cream and I know there is a full tray sitting in the ice-box."

'"There's nothing unusual in fancying some ice-cream, especially on such a warm day as this," I said with what must have been a puzzled expression.

'"Well, I don't want to eat it," smiled the little

32

minx. "Shall I tell you what I want you to do with it?"

'I nodded my assent and Penny ran her pink little tongue round her lips. She smiled and said: "What I would like you to do more than anything else is for you to dip your hands into the soft, rich ice cream and then cover my whole body with it. Smother me all over with the creamy whiteness and let me savour the delicious sensation of the coolness against my hot body. My nipples would be rock-hard and my pussey so hot that the ice-cream would begin to melt and mingle with my cunney juices which would have started to flow. Then I would make you lick all the ice-cream from my body, working slowly down to my titties and across my white belly to my succulent cunt. And when you reach this warm, juicy love-box you lick all round the cunney lips and drive me wild by inserting your cold tongue into my cunt. This would leave me writhing in delight and, oooh, just thinking about this makes me feel so randy. Do you think you could raise your cock again for me?"

'Could I, by Gad! I should say, especially when she lowered her head and sucked its glowing knob with relish, rolling her tongue over the top before taking at least three inches of my shaft into her mouth. So intense were our passions that I knew I would spend unless I took her head away quite quickly. She made no protest when I gently lifted her face upwards but the darling girl turned her lithe body around and stuck her pert, shapely formed bum almost in my face.

'"Ah, Penny, would you like me to fuck your bottom?" I asked, for one should always proceed only with the consent of one's partner as Doctor Stevenson's famous manual tells us. She turned her head and sweetly smiled her agreement. So I clasped my arms around her waist and lightly raised one thigh, guiding the red knob of my prick to her little arsehole. I thrust forward but it would not penetrate and I had no desire to hurt this lovely creature. Sensing my predicament, with her fingers Penny moistened my knob with spittle and again placed it aright; but as it was a somewhat awkward position to lie in, I rolled her on to her belly placing a cushion under her to raise her bum higher. I opened her thighs and this time my prick forced its way between her buttocks. She squirmed and wriggled about, gasping with pleasure to such an extent that I could hardly keep my cock inside her. Her wriggling and the delicious contractions of her bum-hole brought down from me a further copious discharge of frothy white spunk as I frigged her clitty in front, thus procuring her a double pleasure.' As Morris finished his anecdote I noticed Helene Sylvan slip out of the room for what I thought at the time was a call of nature. Meanwhile, the other men were all asking Morris whether Sir Lionel still employed this lovely girl, Penny, in his service.

'Wait, wait a minute. I still have not finished the story!' cried Morris. 'Jenny Everleigh, will you grab Johnny Gerwitz by the balls and plonk him in his chair so that I can continue this tale?'

'I couldn't do that to a member of the nobility,' I said with mock seriousness, 'for it would be a case of *lése majesté*.'

'Don't worry, Jenny,' laughed Captain Gibson, 'the Count is certainly an aristocrat but at my club, The Yencers, he is only a country member.'

'A country member?' I queried.

'Oh, aye,' said the gallant Captain, 'I remember.'

34

Anyways, after some more jocular horsing about Morris continued to tell the enthralled company of his delicious hours spent with Sir Lionel Trapes' maidservant. Clearing his throat, Morris continued: 'Amazingly enough, after a brief respite during which we enjoyed a glass of cold lemonade, we were ready for another bout of *l'amour*.

'Penny kissed my prick again and again and gently eased the now pulsating shaft back into her mouth, sucking furiously, engulfing my entire cock and I was about to roll her over and place my prick in her warm, juicy love-nest when the door was thrown open and who should be there but my old friend Sir Lionel, who had hastened as quickly as he could from his affairs so that he would not be too late for his meeting with me – but I can tell you all something, I wish to hell that he had not worried so much about being late!'

'Tough luck, Morris,' said Beth Pokingham sympathetically, 'as I know to my cost, there is nothing worse than a fuck interrupted halfway through – or in this case, before you had actually begun!'

'How right you are! And I was embarrassed, truth to tell, about being found *in flagrento delecti* by my old friend even though Lionel had obviously set up the situation for me. My erection vanished and I sat up, blinking nervously as the sunlight poured through the open door.

'"Oh dear," said the genial baronet, "I have made a rather unfortunate entrance, have I not – please do not mind me. Do continue your fuck." But despite his urgings and Penny's exquisite attempts to revive my prick with sucking and stroking, I am afraid that I was totally *hors de combat* and I told Penny with regret that this session of lovemaking must come to an end.

35

'"Not to worry sir," said the gorgeous girl brightly, "Sir Lionel or Martin the coachman will fuck me later if I so desire. I do hope that you have enjoyed yourself this afternoon as much as I have and that I have entertained you as well as Sir Lionel had wanted."

'"You earn top marks, my dear," I said and whispered to Lionel if it would be impolite to offer Penny a small monetary gift for all her efforts. "I don't think she would be offended," whispered Lionel so I proffered a five pound note to Polly and said that I hoped she would accept this token of my appreciation in the same spirit as I gave it. "Thank you kindly, sir," she said, pocketing the note, "I will spend some of this on a new summer outfit and make a donation in your name to the Society For Spreading Useful Knowledge Amongst the Leisured Classes."

'"What Society is that?" I asked. "Oh, it is to teach upper crust girls how to fuck," said Sir Lionel cheerily. So I had at least the final satisfaction of contributing to a worthy cause after fucking myself stupid.'

'Well, I don't think the interruption was such a terrible thing,' declared Doctor Stevenson. 'After all that activity, your body needed a rest and I think it was just as well that Sir Lionel came in when he did. How is the old boy by the way? I haven't seen him since that last party Lord Dodder gave at the Connaught Rooms last November.'

But before Morris could answer the doors of the dining room were thrown open and Ronald the footman wheeled in a large silver table set on castors upon which was a cover of a table cloth. Whatever it was under the table cloth seemed to move but what a surprise as Ronald solemnly announced that 'here is a late addition to the menu, ladies and gentlemen', whipping off the cloth to reveal nothing less than the beautiful naked body of Helene Sylvan, the dancer who lay gracefully back covered only by two strawberries smothered in cream that screened her nipples and a delicately laid out little fruit salad of pineapple and peach slices that lay on her forest of glossy black curly hair that extended all over her mount. And topping the magnificent effect was a long banana that stuck out most lasciviously from her cunney lips, causing a thought to flash though my mind almost immediately as to which gentleman would be the first to take that luscious morsel between his lips! Would it be the quiet Doctor Stevenson or the garrulous Morris Cohn-Bickler? Perhaps the handsome Captain Gibson, but no – with an athletic leap that belied his years (for the Count was in his prime), Johnny Gewirtz was up on the table, shucking off his clothes with abandon, pausing only to take off with care his medal ribbon of the Supreme Order of Achanvay, First Class presented to him by Prince Schmockle II of Albania in 1879.

As soon as Ronald placed the tray on the table and discreetly retired from the scene, the Count was between Helene's legs, nibbling and sucking the banana until he reached the glossy black moss of her pubic hair. 'Now for the choicest bites!' he crowed as he kissed and sucked at her oozing pussey. Meanwhile, he flicked the strawberries off her nipples, one landing on the carpet and the other unfortunately right into the left eye of Doctor Stevenson who had been crouching forward to see all the action.

Majestically, Count Gewirtz swooped his arms around the lovely young girl's bum, transferring his face to suck greedily on her engorged, stiff little titties until they stood as erect as two tiny guardsmen. He then kissed his way down, to a round of applause led by Beth Pokingham who was an *aficionado* of well-timed fucking, down Helene's marble white belly to the dark cushion of hair that guarded the entrance to the haven of his desires. He licked his lips in anticipation and his pink tongue extended itself, moving slowly round her puffy cunney lips which caused her to sigh with unashamed delight. Slow yet subtle in his ministrations, the Count parted the lovelips with the very tip of his clever tongue which now sought the moist cleft where already, I was sure Helene's clitty was already swelling.

Her rounded bottom cheeks squirmed around on the table cloth as the Count's tongue lashed juicily around her clitty and we could see the rivulets of love juice spilling down her inner thighs. Her heels drummed against his shoulders as she reached peak after peak of pleasure.

Helene groaned and tossed back her head in delighted frustration. 'Oh fuck me, Johnny! Fuck me now!' she called out and impulsively she stretched out her arms to him, pulling him to her so that his body covered her own and she felt down for the Count's mighty rod that lay sandwiched between their bellies. Johnny was now also consumed with desire and gripping her hips he thrust up without hesitation and I saw an inch or two of his majestic prick sink into her sopping pussey. Helene then whispered something to her love and to a murmur of surprise from the engrossed spectators, the Count withdrew his cock and changed positions with Helene so that he was now flat on his back on the table.

'Why the sudden change, Roy?' muttered Captain Gibson to Doctor Stevenson.

'Ah, I think it is because Helene knows that the Count must be somewhat exhausted. Johnny only arrived in London this morning and at luncheon he was guest of honour at the Jim Jam Club Langtry Society, a select body of gentlemen headed by the Prince of Wales who have enjoyed carnal knowledge of the Jersey Lily. Watch carefully, Jock, for future reference as you may gain some valuable tips about what to do if your lady wants to fuck but you feel rather tired to perform in an over-energetic manner,' replied the good doctor, always a fount of wisdom on matters of an intimate nature.

Helene now was now sitting astride the Count whose noble cock was waving like a flagpole in a high wind. She sat fully astride him, pressing down the lips of her aching slit to the glowing purple dome. She spread her cunney lips apart with her hand and directed the tip of the Count's cock to the gateway of delight and slowly sat down, letting Johnny Gewirtz feel the juices of her warm cunney wash round his willing tool. His hands slid across to her bottom cheeks and Helene wriggled around to work the hard shaft of cock inside her as far up as possible. She bounced merrily away on his iron-hard rod as the Count released her bum cheeks to play with her titties.

'Notice how well this so-called female superior position works,' said Doctor Stevenson quietly, 'and I really do advocate it as an occasional change to one's regular pattern of fucking. It is quite hard work for the girl for unless she has excellent control of her vaginal muscles, she has to lift herself up and down with her legs in rather a cramped position which may set up harmonic motions that may inter- fere with the fucking. Mind you, Helene, being a ballerina means that she has marvellously lithe limbs.'

'I love fucking in this way,' gasped Helene, who had caught the drift of this little dissertation. 'Oooh, it does give my cunt walls a good pounding, especially if the man is as well made as the thick-pricked Count Johnny Gewirtz. Aaaah, that's lovely, I do so enjoy sitting down in this fashion on a stiff cock and grinding my arse around whilst I work my cunney muscles – it gives my clitty a good rub as well!'

She worked her bottom from side to side as the Count jerked his hips up and down and then she caught his rhythm and lifted herself up and down to meet his upward thrusts with downward pushes of her own.

'You see, ladies and gentlemen,' she gasped. 'Oh, Johnny, harder, harder! Oooh! That's so nice! A man normally enjoys this kind of fucking as all he has to do is lie back and watch, though the dear Count is a considerate gentleman who desires to give pleasure – oooh! – as well as to simply receive it. Am I right, Roy?'

'I could not have put it better myself,' said Doctor Stevenson. 'There are lazy, self-indulgent types who only fuck with the girl on top but in my view –'

He was interrupted by a cry of delight from Helene who achieved her orgasm just as the first gushes of cream jetted out from the Count's cock and we heartily applauded the loving couple as they crashed together in a glorious mutual spend.

We then all moved into the lavishly decorated lounge where Aspiso the butler was waiting with more deliciously brewed coffee and liqueurs. Count Gewirtz, having of course hastily put on his clothes, suggested that we all taste kummel, a liqueur very popular in Central and Eastern Europe. 'It is distilled from caraway seeds,' he explained, 'and has undoubted digestive qualities as well as possessing a delicate aroma and quite delicious taste.'

With the exception of Captain Gibson (who stoutly maintained an allegiance to malt whisky from his native land), we all sipped at our drinks and only Beth Pokingham said that she did not enjoy the taste.

'Ah, I am surprised, Beth,' said Count Gewirtz with a smile, 'as kummel is supposed to excite the sexual urges – but then I dare say in your case that is not necessary!'

'Horseshit!' replied Beth somewhat inelegantly, 'I do not believe that you can judge people by what they drink.'

'No, of course not,' I said, 'but did you read the article on colours by Professor Shackleton in *The Times* a few days ago?'

'No, I must have missed it – do tell us about it,' said Helene Sylvan who, having taken a warm bath Ronald the footman had prepared for her (he had been given 'a hand job' as the lower classes put it for his pains), had just entered the room.

'Well, I can best explain his theories like this,' I said, 'tell me, Beth, what is your favourite colour?'

'Blue,' she replied promptly.

'Ah, that somewhat surprises me for blue shows insecurity; the deeper the blue one chooses for a dress, for example, the less confident you must feel. And according to Professor Shackleton, Beth, you like your surroundings to be calm and organized and you need lots of time for rest and recreation. You are a caring person and are very loyal to your friends and can be trusted implicitly to keep confidences. Is this

41

a fair description of you? Perhaps your sister is the best judge. What do you think, Bella?'

'It sounds quite like Beth to me,' she replied cheerily, 'but what about me? My favourite colour is red.'

'The colour of sensuality, I'll be bound,' said Captain Gibson.

'You are quite right, Jock,' I said. 'A preference for red shows an appetite for fucking but although it shows a need for romance it also shows a desire for change and for the need to stay in control of a situation. According to the Professor, Bella, it also shows that you enjoy social intercourse and are naturally gregarious and on the negative side, you lack a sense of purpose. You need to find a good cause and throw yourself into it.'

'Would my bed qualify?' quipped Morris Cohn-Bickler. 'Anyhow, I don't know what your professor would say about my favourite colour – because it's black!'

'Well, he would say that you crave power, Morris, and that you are quite single-minded in your determination to achieve it. You rarely disengage from the fray and hold strong opinions as you believe that the world is a cold, tough place so you must temper your nature accordingly.'

'I wouldn't say I'm a cold person,' he protested, 'though I cannot deny that I am absolutely determined to better myself. My parents fled to this country as penniless refugees from the Czar's pogroms and I have always had to have extra strength to claw my way up the ladder. Even here, people of my persuasion have to fight against prejudice as they do all over Europe as Johnny Gewirtz will surely testify.'

'Yes, of course, but you'd still be a sharp bastard even if you were the Archbishop of Warsaw!' said the Count. 'Come now, how about me, Jenny, my favourite colour is silver.'

'An interesting choice,' I said. 'It shows that you are a man to shy away from personal commitments – this must be true as you have never married.'

'Well, why should he – the man fucks his way round the courts of Europe and the best houses in North America,' said Morris, unwittingly proving Professor Shackleton's theory.

'Maybe so,' I continued, 'but he has had so many chances to be betrothed that I think the Professor's views hold water. Oh, the choice of silver also shows that although Johnny is mechanically minded, if there is any really hard physical work to be done, he will always employ somebody else to undertake it!'

Bella Pokingham finished her coffee and said: 'I don't know whether I believe all that business about colours. It all sounds like fortune-telling to me. Isn't it time we began to play some party games? Or shall I first tell you a story to put you all in the mood?'

'I'm game,' said her sister, 'and I'm sure that Helene and Jenny are ready for a fuck. But you know how lazy the men are – Bella, tell the company about the experience you enjoyed the other weekend at Lord and Lady Albion's country manor.'

'Oh, yes,' laughed Bella, 'I shall enjoy recounting this true story. Although Beth and I had both been invited to the Albions' Somerset house, Beth had a slight indisposition so I went alone. Unfortunately, I was partnered with Sir Peter Wright, the famous explorer and naturalist. We were pushed together by accident as his wife was away at some conference on helping Kensington unfortunates. However, all he talked about was his recent trip to Antarctica and his study of penguins and showed no interest in fucking.

'So I went to bed alone feeling very frustrated as I had not enjoyed a good, stiff cock up my cunt for at least two weeks. My current beau, Sir Martin Wellsend, had been called away to his Scottish estates and I do so miss his luscious cock sliding into my tight, wet pussey.

'Anyway, I undressed slowly and padded into the bathroom. I ran a nice, hot bath and settled in for a long, relaxing soak when I heard sounds coming from the other side of the wall. It turned out that this wall was a new, thin division between two new bathrooms Lord Albion had only recently installed and I could quite plainly hear sounds of giggling and splashing. I kept listening and the giggling turned into little gasps and then little yelps of delight as my neighbour (whom I knew to be Estelle de Quentonne, one of the belles of Parisian Society) was obviously enjoying a lovely fucking in her bath with the Honourable Harry Wharton, the young lover she had brought down for the weekend.

'I was getting a little excited listening to this girl having one orgasm after another but I wasn't quite in the mood to play with myself. I stepped out of the bath and dried off and then looked at my reflection in the mirror. My large breasts stood firmly on my bosom and the brisk towelling had popped my pert, pink nipples out. I had recently shaved my pussey and the pink lips looked soft and damp. I gingerly touched myself and found that my cunney was soaked so I supposed that listening to Estelle had excited me more than I thought.

'I suddenly noticed a folder on the bedside table

that had obviously been left in error by the last house-guest. I opened it and saw that there were several photographs inside it. Good heavens, I thought to myself, could these be photographs by Henry Sailor, the well-known photographer of the nude form who I knew had been staying here recently.

'To my joy, I found that I was indeed in luck and that these were indeed samples of the recherché photographs that have made Sailor's name so famous in and around Mayfair. [Editor's Note – "Henry Sailor" is a lightly disguised pseudonym for the real-life Victorian photographer Henry Hayler who established an extremely lucrative business in pornographic photographs in the 1880s. Many were sold by his friend John Camden Hotten from his tiny bookshop in Piccadilly. Like the men behind the infamous Cleveland Street club for upper-class homosexuals, Hayler had bribed the police well enough to continue in business for many years. When pressure was finally put on Scotland Yard to close down Hayler's premises, the photographer was warned three days beforehand by the police. Nevertheless, although Hayler was given ample time to arrange his affairs before fleeing to the Continent, the police raid netted more than 130,000 photographic negatives and more than 5,000 glass lantern-slides. Hayler destroyed his lists of customers and lived quietly off his considerable fortune until his death in 1902.]

'I looked through the photographs which set my blood boiling. The first showed a pretty young girl sucking a cock whilst another man was inserting his prick into her pussey from behind. The second showed her handling the prick she had just sucked as the frothy white spunk jetted from the top whilst in

45

the third photograph she was seen cramming both pricks into her mouth. I could almost taste the salty cream that Martin produces for me whilst we are engaged in *l'arte de faire l'amour*.

'Just at this time I heard even louder noises coming from next door where Estelle was screaming and Harry was bellowing like a foghorn. This was all too much to bear and I threw myself down and spread my legs wide. I slid three fingers inside my soaking love-channel and used the other hand to caress my tits. I glanced up at the reflection on the ceiling and was overcome by the incredible sight. The naughty Lord Albion had installed a mirror there so I could see myself masturbating – something I had never been able to do before and I watched quite mesmerized as I slid my glistening fingers in and out and began to rub my swollen clitty.

'My body was becoming hotter by the second and my breathing was coming in gasps as the heat from my pussey increased. I felt the first faint waves of orgasm start deep inside but they soon began to spread and were soon thundering through me, setting every nerve in my body on fire with intense passion and pleasure. At the same time, Estelle and Harry were coming together and their cries and gasps made me even hornier and my orgasm got stronger and stronger. I finally stopped spending after blissfully long seconds of the most intense pleasure.

'When I arrived back in Berkeley Square I telephoned Martin and told him to put a mirror on the ceiling in his bedroom. The dear boy agreed to my request and that night we enjoyed a tremendous bout of fucking. The sight in the mirror of his massive cock slipping into my cunt was so amazingly exciting. Unfortunately, I do not think Papa and

Mama would give their consent for Aspiso to put a mirror on my own bedroom ceiling!'

This stirring tale certainly had the desired effect upon the gentlemen. Notwithstanding his previous cavorting with Helene Sylvan on the dining room table, Count Gewirtz was ready and eager for the fray – only this time with myself as his partner.

We embraced passionately and he quickly raised my petticoats and dress and soon my drawers were down to my ankles. Without further ado he covered my mouth with a burning kiss and slid his hands between my legs, feeling my hairy slit, tickling my clitty and rousing all my warming passions. I began to squirm with delight as the Count tenderly opened the yielding lips of my crack, sliding his fingers into my dainty quim that was already moistening to a delicious wetness. As he frigged me with one, two and then three fingers, I took hold of his thick prick, which he had released from the confines of his trousers, and taking hold of this monstrous weapon with both hands, I lowered my pretty mop of curls to receive the red dome between my pouting lips. This was the first aristocratic cock I had ever sucked and funnily enough it felt and tasted differently from my boy friend, Johnny Oaklands' or that of the randy American dentist Ronnie Donne. For a start it was so smooth and when I pushed back the skin it was all I could do to get the rich ruby dome into my mouth. I ran my tongue round it and licked off some juice which had already formed there. I ran my mouth down the whole length of his shaft and sucked his balls which were as big as the largest eggs. I sucked on this great monster with relish, my soft tongue rolling over and over the dome but then the Count pulled back as he had felt the beginnings of a spend and he had no wish to close proceedings so quickly.

We threw off our clothes in gay abandon and he then lay down and made me kneel over his face which enabled him to lick the inside of my thighs, teasing me by going right up to my labia and then away again. Eventually he did start to lap my cunney lips which opened for him to tongue my clitty which drove me to a glorious madness.

I could contain myself no longer and I rolled off him onto my back. The Count was now kneeling in front of me and I felt a hand thoughtfully placing two plumped up cushions under my buttocks. The hand belonged to Beth Pokingham who wriggled round to slip her hands underneath the Count's balls which she squeezed gently. She then kindly guided his cock into my aching cunney. I had obviously aroused Johnny Gewirtz to a frenzy for he set off on a gallop as fast as a jockey at Goodwood Races. I clung to him as best I could, bucking my hips urgently so as not to be left behind. I lifted my bottom, rotating my hips as fast as I could to achieve the maximum contact.

No-one could last such a frenzied pace and the Count groaned and stiffened as I felt his fingernails digging into my back. Fortunately, my own spend was already boiling up inside me as his prick gushed out an enormous torrent of spunk inside my pussey as my cunt nipped and contracted on his throbbing cock. I came just as his dear prick began to contract and we collapsed down on the carpet together, exhausted but well satisfied.

'Oh dear,' said the Count, 'I fear my spunk and your love-juices Jenny have stained the carpet.'

'Not to worry, Johnny,' said Bella, 'I'll have

Aspiso dab at it with a little of Lady Jemima Gaffney's special spot remover. It has never failed yet, has it, Jock?'

'Indeed not,' said the gallant Scotchman, 'why, only last week after a particularly eventful fuck with Lady Blintzer, Doctor Arkley and myself, we had to clean the bedroom wall as well as the carpet and her magic bottle of cleansing liquid did the trick quite beautifully.'

Our fucking had excited all the other members of the company who followed our example and undressed so that we were now all in the nude. 'I hope you are not too tired, Jenny,' said Bella Pokingham, 'as I would like to eat your pussey.'

'Be *my* guest as I have already been yours this evening,' I replied and stretched myself out ready to resume my erotic games.

Bella sank to her knees on the thickly piled light blue carpet in front of me and without ado buried her pretty face in my dripping pussey. She flicked her tongue back and forth across my already swollen clitty and I must confess that, as I had noticed before, girls know far better than most men how to suck pussey. Oh, the pleasure was so sweet it was almost unbearable.

'I do believe that I am going to spend straight away,' I breathed, clutching the back of her head as she continued to lick and lap at my clitty.

'Well, we can't have that now, can we,' she smiled and raising her head, she climbed on top of me so that our two naked bodies were rubbing together cheek by jowl, or rather in this case tittie to tittie and pussey to pussey.

She began to fondle my waiting breasts and swirled my hardened nipples in her mouth, sending chills of

49

desire up and down my spine. She slid her fingers down my body with gentle, titillating strokes.

Despite the presence of spectators, the walls of taboo had been shattered and I welcomed eagerly Bella's sensuous touch and I felt myself becoming more aroused with each caress. As her knowing fingers inched towards my cunney I felt my thighs stiffen and my hips involuntarily thrust forward in tantalising anticipation of what was to come. Bella dipped her finger through my blonde downy moss and settled on my pussey lips around which she drew hard little circles until I was squirming with pleasure. And she followed this by slipping two fingers into my soaking opening.

'Oh, Bella! That's marvellous!' I whispered as I grabbed her shoulders to pull her even closer towards me.

'Touching you like this makes my pussey so wet,' she replied softly, 'feel me, I'm dripping for you.'

She led my hand down between her silky, firm thighs and then she began kissing my titties, my tummy and then down back again to lap at my wet cunt. Then suddenly she stopped and I opened my eyes wide in shocked disappointment. But she sensed my worry and said: 'Just lie back Jenny, my sister Beth and I have a surprise for you.'

And she took a silver cigar box from her sister, opening it to reveal an exquisitely formed rubber two headed dildo – moulded, as I later found out, by Lady Moser from the magnificent prick of my old friend Nathan Wabolowski.

She also took out of the box a small jar of cherry-flavoured oil which she poured liberally all over the dildo and then dribbled the last drain on my already sopping pussey.

Bella went back to work on my cunney with her mouth, but now she added the dildo, pressing it gently to my pussey lips, working in slowly until it filled me as completely as Count Johnny Gewirtz's cock. She stopped lapping at my clitty and pulled herself up until she was sitting astride my thighs. Our eyes locked as I watched her finger herself with one hand whilst she vibrated the rubber prick in my cunney with the other.

When her own cunt was juicy she raised herself up, slowly working the exposed other part of the dildo into her pussey. She reached for me and pulled me forward until we were pressed together, tittie to tittie, cunt to cunt.

I wrapped my legs as tightly as I could round her back and she wrapped hers round mine and rocking back and fourth, we achieved a rhythm that sent pulses of pleasure to every nerve centre in my body. As our excitement grew, our motions became even more frenzied.

'Oh, Bella, Bella, fuck me! Oooh! This is so lovely, don't stop, don't stop!' I screamed.

'I won't, I won't, Jenny, darling! Aaaah! Aaaah! How divine, how scrumptious! Do it more! More!' panted Bella as we continued to fuck ourselves as the magical dildo prodded through our cunnies, nipping its way along the velvety grooves as we arched our bodies in ecstasy. Here were two girls literally fucking each other so perfectly that together our bodies started to shudder and our heads thrashed about as we swam in a veritable sea of lubricity, almost swooning with the pleasure of our frenzied emissions.

We lay there for some moments, pressed together, our cunts joined by the rubber dildo of which only a fraction of an inch was visible to Captain Gibson who, squatting down beside us, used his long tapering fingers to finger out the heads from our cunts to separate us.

Watching our sensual display had certainly affected Doctor Stevenson who asked Beth to kneel down beside her sister, thus affording me a grandstand view of Beth's lovely rounded bum cheeks. Beth did as she was told and wriggled herself onto her belly, sticking up her bottom provocatively. Bella leaned up to take hold of Doctor Stevenson's thickly erect prick and placed it lasciviously at the entrance to her sister's puckered rosette.

'Go on, Roy, go on,' smiled Beth, turning her face round and upwards to the doctor, 'I want a nice big pressing of juice up my arse.'

She wriggled as the doctor pushed his huge knob between her buttocks but soon she was responding gaily to every shove and I could see and hear Roy's heavy balls bouncing against Beth's smooth, round bottom as her arse-cheeks were drawn irresistibly tight against his commendably flat belly. He moved in and out in a slow, shunting movement, snaking his right hand round her waist and diving into her dark, curly motte. I moved my hand up to massage Beth's sopping pussey, giving her the double pleasure of a fuck from both in front and behind. This brought Roy to the boil quite quickly and with an almighty thrust he spurted into her, working his truncheon back and forth to warm and lubricate Beth's superb backside. His cock was still stiff when with a quite audible 'pop' he uncorked it from her well-lubricated bum-hole.

'Ah, Beth,' said the author of the world famous manual on fucking, 'Your bum remains one of the nicest fucks in the whole country.'

'How kind of you to say so,' said Beth, 'for I value your opinion. Mind, without wishing to be immodest, the playwright Mr Oscar Wilde has said much the same thing but I sometimes wonder whether his tastes are really for pansy boys as he shows little interest in my cunt.'

'The man's a turd, then,' said Captain Gibson forcefully, giving his enormous Scottish cock a few rubs to bring it up to its fullest height. 'Let me pay homage, Beth, to your lovely cunney.'

In a trice he was on the carpet with her, his hands moving over her aroused body with practiced ease. He squeezed her rather large yet firm breasts and rubbed the big, dark nipples against his palms making them flash up into little stalks. He then began to kiss her body from the forehead downwards, finally arriving at her open pussey. I could smell her cunney from where I was lying, not more than nine inches away. She smelled really nicely, with a spicy tang that had my own mouth watering.

But it was Jock Gibson who was to fuck Beth's lovely pussey. She guided his magnificent prick into what must have been the wettest pussey so far that evening. She wrapped her arms and legs around the gallant captain and urged him to make it 'Hard and fast, Jock – don't wait.'

'As you wish,' growled the Edinburgh cocksman, kissing her breasts and belly a second time and then prising open her pussey lips with his fingers, sinking them slowly into her slit which was already dribbling with juice. She reached out and squeezed one of her titties as he slowly moved on top of her and she responded excitedly, opening her legs wide and clamping her feet round his back as he guided his throbbing prick into her soaking little nookie. She took up the rhythm of his thrusts and I could see Beth's legs shake and tremble and knew that she would soon be spending.

This erotic spectacle was too much for Morris Cohn-Bickler to bear and he grabbed hold of his erect cock, pulling his fist up and down the swollen shaft. 'Join in, Morris, join in!' cried Captain Gibson but as Morris knelt down to insert his cock into Beth's willing mouth he could no longer contain himself and he pumped spurt after spurt of hot sticky cream over the entwined lovers, who oblivious to their coating of jism, were still jerking, panting and thrusting. The end was near now, though, and after a brace of marvellously powerful surging strokes of his cock, they shouted together with joy in their mutual climax, the Captain pumping jet after jet of juice into her eager crack, her hands gripping his sizeable bum-cheeks, pushing him deeper and deeper inside her until they collapsed, utterly exhausted in a tangle of limbs on the carpet which was by now in urgent need of a libation of Lady Gaffney's special cleaner.

'I am surprised you can spend so easily, Beth,' said Helene Sylvan as we refreshed ourselves with the ices Aspiso had left on the sideboard, 'as I don't think you have had the pleasure of being fucked by Captain Gibson before this evening. Myself, I find it somewhat difficult to spend with men that I don't know very well.'

'On the whole, I also find it difficult,' agreed Beth, 'and for the first fuck I often prefer the Eastern position where the man is sitting down with his feet crossed and you sit on his cock and you have your feet round his back. You only have to rock a bit for your clitty to be stimulated and you can really concentrate on each other,' replied Beth.

'Yes, I like that way too,' I said, 'though I'm not inhibited and I really like to jump around and grab hold of my man's cock. I like to put it in my cunney and to hold his balls whilst we are fucking, just like you were doing, Helene, with Johnny Gewirtz.'

'Yes, well, the Count is a very good lover. Did you notice the way he executed those long, thrilling strokes? My cunney felt like a violin and the Count's cock was like the bow and every stroke raised the most ravishing melody on my senses that could possibly be imagined!'

'I am so pleased you enjoyed it so much,' said Count Gewirtz proudly, 'I am always at your service, Helene, as I am at the service of all the ladies present.'

'All four of us?' asked Bella mischievously.

'Without distinction,' he promptly replied, 'and at the same time if you so desire.'

'But excellent though it is, you have only one cock!' cried Beth.

'Would you like me to demonstrate?' he said, smiling broadly, 'Come here, Jenny, help me begin the game and I'll call you other ladies to participate as soon as possible.'

I'm always game for a new erotic adventure so I took the Count's hand and he put me on my knees in front of him.

'Suck my prick, please, Jenny, so we can begin the proceedings,' commanded the Count.

I did as I was told but after giving the swelling shaft a gentle squeeze, I sucked the red mushroomed knob slowly, taking more and more gently into my mouth, licking and lapping at the thick cock, savouring every inch. I'm afraid I slurped rather noisily as my head moved back and forth until I felt that the Count's cock was at peak condition.

He then moved quickly, pulling me down onto the carpet (more work for Lady Gaffney's mixture! I thought fleetingly) and pulling my legs onto his shoulders, he slid his huge prick deep inside me. He buried himself inside my cunt with a deep, strong thrust that almost mashed my clitty against his pubic bone but my juices were flowing freely as he held very still which made me spend even more.

When my spasms stopped and I lay there perspiring and gasping for breath, he began to stroke into me, moving with lightning force and speed for perhaps as long as a minute until I spent. Then he would stop and hold his stiff cock inside me quite still until the orgasm passed. He did this three times until, without missing a beat, he rolled over onto his back, his cock still inside me, so that now I was on top.

'Come here, Helene, and sit on my face!' he called to the petite ballerina. She obeyed with alacrity, straddling his face and facing me so that he could lick her cunt. Fired by this idea, Helene and I kissed passionately and played with each other's erect nipples. And without being called, the Pokingham sisters lay down beside the Count, fingering their cunnies in excitement until he extended both his arms to dip each hand into each girl's sopping pussey and thus bringing all four girls to a glorious mutual spend.

To add to the tableau, Doctor Stevenson and Morris Cohn-Bickler lay on top of Beth and Bella Pokingham respectively and fucked their pussies properly with their pricks as Captain Gibson, still *hors de combat* from his previous exercise, opened the door and bellowed to Aspiso to bring in another magnum of champagne.

Could there be a finer climax to an evening's entertainment? I must confess that we played further games until well into the small hours. The champagne fired all the members of the company to further feats and I well remember the formulation of a superb fucking chain with Doctor Stevenson fucking Beth whilst having Bella work her dildo into her sister's bottom as she sucked the thick prick of Captain Gibson, who in turn was finger fucking Helene who was licking my clitty whilst having Count Gewirtz insert his cock into her tight little bum hole.

The party broke about just before one o'clock in the morning and Graeme, my faithful coachman was on hand to take me back to South Kensington. As you know, diary, I slept like a log and Connor made sure that the servants performed their work as quietly as possible until I came down for breakfast at the quite disgraceful hour of half past ten o'clock! What happened later that day I shall recount a new entry for I am still somewhat tired from my exertions chez Pokingham and I need a lazy day to recover.


*25 September 1889*
This morning Holly Digweed called round for morning coffee. I do not know of anyone so aptly named for although Holly is an attractive girl of nineteen, to my mind she lives and breathes only for horticulture.

After some perfunctory small talk Holly asked me whether I had yet visited the beautiful gardens at Nymans House owned by the Messel family.

'You really should go, Jenny,' she said earnestly, 'as the gardens are quite magnificent. Are you familiar with the house?'

'No, I don't think I know of it,' I said.

'My dear Jenny, you really must go there,' she continued, 'it is only some thirty miles from London on the Brighton Road near the little village of Hand-cross.

'The gardens cover some thirty acres and Mr Messel is making Nymans a real showcase with many rare conifers, shrubs and other plants which have been gathered from all over the world.'

'How fascinating,' I said, trying hard to keep the signs of boredom from my voice.

'Why not come down with us the day after tomorrow, Jenny? I am arranging a small party and I need another girl to make up the numbers. Sir Andrew Scott will be accompanying me – I think you know Andrew, he was at the Herts and Middlesex Hunt Ball as a guest of the Master, grumpy old Major Cosgrave. And the other man is a Swedish agricultural scientist, Martin Breslau, whose company I am sure you will enjoy.'

'Will I, Holly? I'm not that interested in flowers to be absolutely truthful.'

'Ah, but Martin is a handsome young brute so if you don't like looking at the beauties of nature you can always look at him!'

'That makes a difference, Holly, I must admit! But I don't speak any Swedish.'

'You silly thing, the Swedes all speak English, often just as well if not better than we do. Do say you'll come.'

I looked at the pages of my appointments book and as the page for Thursday was blank, I decided to accept Holly's kind invitation. The weather was fine and the forecast was set fair so what had I to lose? Who knows, this Swedish gentleman might prove to be a most agreeable companion so if Dame Fortune were to smile upon me, a previously blank day may hold some unknown, hidden delights.


*28 September 1889*

> Let those who never tried, believe,
>   In women's chastity!
> Let Her who ne'er was asked, receive
>   The praise of modesty!
>
> Tho' woman's virtue's true as steel
>   Before you touch her soul;
> Still let it once the magnet feel
>   'Twill flutter towards the Pole!
>         *Sir Lionel Trapes*
>         [1826–1908]

What a splendid day in the country, diary, I spent yesterday with Holly Digweed and two gentlemen, previously unknown to me but now close, *close* friends. How pleased I am that I took up Holly's kind invitation – the episode proves beyond doubt that one should never sit back and wait for happiness. Far better to stir oneself and go out looking for this elusive quality. It's strange, really, how often I have looked forward with intense eagerness to a particular event and how often the day or evening has somehow failed to live up to expectation. Conversely, when I have only mildly welcomed certain happenings, they have often turned out to be the most enjoyable, and yesterday's outing to Nymans Gardens was certainly a fine example of this as I was not looking forward to the outing very much yet I had a lovely time!

Holly's coach called for me at half past ten in the morning and we stopped off at Sir Andrew Scott's Knightsbridge *pied a terre* where he and Martin Breslau were waiting for us. The party should have been six-handed but Alexandra Cox and her latest *amour* Jack Worthing had been called to the bedside of Jack's Uncle Algy who was apparently at death's door.

Sir Andrew and Mister Breslau were waiting on the pavement as we approached Paterson Mews and Holly made the introductions as we sped off as fast as the traffic would allow towards Victoria. The clever girl had arranged for a coach from her Aunt Augusta (who lived only six miles from Handcross) to meet us at the station and be at our disposal for the rest of the day.

As Holly had told me, I had met Sir Andrew before and I must say that I was impressed with the bearing of the lean young baronet. Sir Andrew was known as something of an aesthete having essays published in Blackwoods, two poems in the The Gentleman's Magazine and also – though I did not find this out until later in the day – had composed a poem that had been printed in *The Oyster*, the salacious publication that many of my gentlemen friends keep hidden in their bedroom cabinets!

It was soon apparent to me that Holly had designs upon Sir Andrew's body for she sat next to him and placed her hand on his thigh quite openly as we drove to Victoria Station. So the pretty girl does think about rosy pricks as much as she does about prickly roses, I mentally noted, but this pleased me as I had no desire myself to compete for Sir Andrew's cock as I was very taken by the handsome Martin Breslau who sat beside me. He was a tall young man, well over six foot in height, as fair-haired as I am, with the blue eyes and light colouring we expect of the Scandinavian races. He was well-covered though by no means plump and possessed a charming manner which quite swept me off my feet.

There is something about a railway compartment, diary, that excites my sensual appetite. [Editor's Note: In *The Intimate Memoirs of Dame Jenny Everleigh 4: The Secret Diaries*, Jenny recounts an orgiastic experience with two other young ladies on a train going up to London from the West Country whilst in *5: The American Dream* she sets down her memories of an extraordinary sex party on the New York to Washington railroad.]

We had no sooner settled into our private compartment when Sir Andrew, ever the forward young spark, said to Holly: 'Well now, my dear, has any lucky cock found its way up your cranny lately?'

'How rude of you, Andrew,' I scolded, 'for shame speaking in such bold fashion in front of two ladies and a gentleman from another country. Whatever will he think of our English manners?'

'Oh, do not trouble on my account, Jenny,' said Martin cheerfully. 'In Sweden we are far more forthright than you British when it comes to social and sexual intercourse.'

And to my astonishment Holly chipped in: 'It is very sweet of you, Jenny, but I don't mind telling Andrew details of my intimate life. It makes me feel very happy and I know how much it excites him from the size of the bulge in the front of his trousers! So as you have no objection, my dear, I will gladly answer Andrew's question on one condition.'

'Oh-ho, and just what condition might that be?' said the gay baronet.

61

'Simply that you tell us whose pussey your prick has been visiting lately – presuming that you have been fortunate enough to find a lady kind enough to allow you to lodge Mr Pego in her little lodge.'

'Fair enough, I'll tell all but you must begin the game,' grinned Andrew.

'As you wish,' said Holly, 'if you are all sitting comfortably, I'll begin. If you really want to know, my last fuck was on last Sunday afternoon.

'You will recall that last Sunday was an uncommonly warm day and I spent the day with Papa and Mama at our country home near the aptly named village of Gobblecock – the place is aptly named as the grocer's wife was found sucking off the Vicar in the vestry last June but that is another story – and I decided to spend the early afternoon walking through the lush, green grass of Webb's Meadow. It was so warm that I had slipped off all my clothes except for a thin white cotton dress through which, I had little doubt, the generous contours of my breasts and bum could easily be seen in the great shafts of golden light from the sun that was shining almost overhead.

'It was such a pleasant experience walking barefoot, my hair cascading down my shoulders, that I wandered unthinking and uncaring towards Goldhill Wood. My eyes were half closed in the bright sunshine and it was entirely my fault that I bumped right into a young man who was coming out of the wood in order to reach the village road through the track that Farmer Webb had laid through his field.

'"Oh, I do beg you pardon," I exclaimed, "I was simply not looking where I was going."

'"That's alright Miss Holly, ma'am, think nothing of it," said a boyish voice and I looked up to see just who I had bumped into. To my not unpleasant surprise, I had cannoned into Leon Wingate, the head boy of Nottsgrove Academy, the progressive boarding-school whose grounds bordered Farmer Webb's land. I had met Leon briefly on a previous occasion back in May when the Principal of Nottsgrove Academy, Doctor Simon White had invited local ladies and gentlemen of quality to a tea-party at the School. Leon was only seventeen and a half years old – almost three years my junior – but he was a very good-looking boy, tall for his age, slimly built but with a fine physique. I had only seen him the once when he was dressed in the Nottsgrove summer uniform but on this sultry September afternoon, he was clad only in running singlet and shorts.

'"It is Leon Wingate, is it not? You are the captain of Nottsgrove, I believe? You obviously remember me as you knew my name."

'"Of course I remembered your name. How could I ever forget the name of the beautiful girl who stole my heart and the heart of every red-blooded boy in the Sixth Form when you visited the Academy last May?"

'What a gallant speech from the young scamp! I could not help blushing slightly and I said that I hoped I had not interfered with an athletic event of some kind in which he might be taking part.

'"I wouldn't care a jot even if you had," he replied, "but the truth is that I thought I would go out for a walk and I simply put on my gymnastic outfit as the weather was so deucedly hot."

'"It most certainly is warm," I said boldly, "Why don't we sit down and enjoy this beautiful day together?"

'"I would adore that, Miss Holly," he said, beaming all over his face. "How lucky I am that I decided

63

to relieve myself in Goldhill Wood for otherwise I would not have had the pleasure of being bumped into by you!"

'We laughed and taking his hand, I motioned him to sit down upon a nearby hummock of earth. We sat in silence for a minute or two and I enjoyed the sensation of having the earth pressed into my cunney. I leaned back against a tree trunk, opening my legs wide so that the sun shone warmly on my pussey and I knew full well that Leon could easily make out the outlines of its dark, curly hair in the glistening light.

'I closed my eyes, allowing the warmth to seep through me, filling me with an acute and sensuous awareness of my own physical being. I moved my hand lazily across my thigh and then, to the boy's intense delight, let my fingers slip across to his knee, running them up to his hips and down again, and I could see the first stirrings of movement in his groin.

'"Do you like that, Leon?" I asked somewhat unnecessarily as he sighed with delight as I let my fingers stray across his tummy and down between his legs where a sizeable bulge was now straining the white cotton material.

'"Oh, Miss Holly, that's absolutely terrific. Oh goodness, I'm, oh gosh, my, er, –"  The dear lad stopped in blushing confusion, putting his hand between his legs. "I am sorry, I'm afraid I –"

'"Heavens alive, Leon, what are you worried about? I should hope that you would get a hard-on after I stroked you down there."

'A sudden thought struck me – was this handsome lad still a virgin? The idea whetted my appetite enormously and I asked him to look me straight in the eyes and tell me truthfully as to whether he had yet been initiated into the joys of *l'arte de faire l'amour*.

I could not resist licking my lips as Leon blurted out that he had not as yet crossed the sexual Rubicon.

'"This is nothing to be ashamed of, my love," I murmured, "Why, stuck in this school at least fifty miles from London, what chance have you to find yourself a girl-friend?"

'"It's kind of you to say so, Miss Holly," he said quietly, "although some of us have found willing girls in the village. Young Sayers, for example, has screwed at least four of the maids at Squire Loring's mansion."

'"Good heavens, are you sure? All men tend to exaggerate their prowess in these matters."

'"Maybe, maybe – but I heard two of the girls talk about him whilst out walking a couple of weeks ago and they were marvelling at how he manages to keep his instrument as stiff as a board even after the completion of his injections."

'I must confess to making a mental note to arrange a meeting with young Sayers for a hard man is good to find – one always meets the other kind more often than not. But I digress – I pulled Leon down until we were both lying down together and then I stretched my legs out in front of me leaving them wide apart. I pushed up my dress so that it lay in a cotton pile just above my bare pussey and his face moved closer to mine so that I could feel his urgent breathing in my ear.

'Now totally aroused, I took my dress in both hands and lifted it up over my head so that I now lay totally naked before him. His fingers lightly brushed my breasts and my nipples immediately jumped to attention.

'"Do you like my titties, Leon?" I whispered into

65

his ear, "why don't you suck them for me, there's a good boy."

'His mouth came down to meet the soft flesh, his hands gently pushing my breasts together as his tongue came forward to circle around my engorged nipples. Then his mouth opened and drew in the soft flesh, his tongue constantly moving, sending wild vibrations through my whole body. Then I guided his hand down over my white belly to my hairy pussey and I let his fingers caress my pubic bush.

'My cunney fairly throbbed, pulsing my juices from me in a hot, sticky wetness. His mouth was now on my titties again, his tongue reaching out to slide wickedly round my nipples as his hand now moved in and out of my thoroughly wet cunt until he was sliding his fingers around my pulsating clitty, pressing it and releasing it in a throbbing movement and my juices were now flowing freely as he inserted first one, then two and finally three fingers up and into me. Leon may have never fucked before but he had (as he later confessed) petted with Polly, the assistant matron at Nottsgrove who had showed him how to handle a lady and had on occasion rubbed his prick up to boiling point though she had never let him spend for fear of marking the clean clothes.

'My back arched with ecstacy as the boy's skilful fingers slithered over my clitty, sending me into deliriums of pure joy. Now was the time to reciprocate, and I moved my hands across to his hips and pulled down his shorts as he took his own hand away from my pussey to pull his singlet over his head so that now he too was naked. I gasped when I saw the size of his bare cock for it must have been quite seven or even eight inches long and of a substantial thickness.

66

'"What a delicious looking cock," I said, smacking my lips, "how exciting to think that I shall be the very first girl to suck it."

'I moved forward and brought my lips down onto this monster and I let my tongue run the full length of the shaft, running back to the knob to catch a hot, sticky drip of spend that had formed at the "eye" of the purple mushroomed dome. I ran my lips around the tip and then opened my mouth to accept its entrance. In a single movement he forced at least three inches of hot prick into my mouth and my body jerked instinctively away from the utter force of it. He retracted slightly so that it lay motionless, though throbbing on my tongue. I closed my lips around the monster sweetmeat and moved my tongue across its width. I sucked greedily on his lovely big prick and twisted Leon's head down so that his face was pushed into my own sopping groin and my body shook with delight as the clever boy realised what he had to do and began circling his tongue around my dripping crack.

'I felt his mouth flick across the grooves of my cunt setting off new tingling waves of pleasure. I just had to have his cock inside me now so I gently raised his head and then taking his cock in my hands I said, rather pompously I suppose looking back over the incident: "Now Leon, this is the moment of truth. You are about to fuck your first girl and I am honoured to be the first recipient of your frothy white semen!"

'He needed no further urging, that's for sure, and he rolled on top of me as I spread my legs as wide as possible, keeping my hands on his prick to guide him into my yearning pussey. Heavens, his thick cock felt quite incredible as he pounded into me with the

67

exciting speed and power one would expect of a first-timer. Naturally enough he spent almost immediately, shooting jets of hot, creamy spunk into my waiting cunney, but the young rascal was able to keep his stiffness even after he had spent and this time I decided to keep the fucking going for a longer period of time. So directly every inch of Leon's monster cock was inside me and our pubic hairs were entwining together, I closed my thighs, making the handsome boy open his own legs and lie astride me with his prick sweetly trapped inside my cunt.

'Leon could not move his prick forwards or backwards as the muscles of my cunt were gripping him so tightly, but then I ground my hips round, massaging his shaft as it throbbed powerfully inside my juicy love-channel which was dribbling juices all down my thighs. He grasped my bum cheeks which I absolutely adore so I eased the pressure round his prick very slightly and he began to drive wildly in and out, again fucking at a truly incredible speed. My pussey clamped down in a final burst of ecstacy as his stiff, jerking prick shot massive wads of hot cream deep inside me. I pushed my pussey up against him, burying his cock even deeper and just let all that wonderful froth bathe my inner walls until my whole body glowed with lust.

'We lay still for a minute or two and then Leon slowly pulled out and sat up, gasping for breath. I bent down and licked his lovely cock clean, savouring the taste of his cream and my own tangy juices. Luckily I had a handkerchief in my dress pocket so I cleaned my pussey up as best I could before we slipped back into our clothes to beat a hasty retreat for we both realised that somebody from Nottsgrove or the village could easily walk by.

'Leon begged me to let him fuck me again but I think it best if he meets some different girls now that he has gained some valuable experience. And frankly, the dear boy is too young for me. I thoroughly enjoyed the episode and I am sure that he will never forget his introduction to fucking. But both he and I need to meet new partners with whom we can enjoy longer, more complete relationships which ultimately are far more satisfying than "one-off" fucks.'

What a smashing yarn, I thought, and I felt like breaking the silence in the carriage as Holly finished her story with a round of applause.

Sir Andrew let out his breath and spoke for all of us when he said: 'Holly, what a marvellously exciting lascivious tale. I don't really think that I can match you either in content or in the terrific way that you bring the story to life.'

'No, no, you must now don the storyteller's mantle,' Holly protested. 'I am sure that you can do just as well and look, the train is slowing down. Do you remember, there was a notice chalked up at Victoria warning us of some delays on the line as workmen are repairing some track. Come on, Andrew, it is your turn to keep us entertained.'

'Is this the wish of you two as well?' asked Sir Andrew, turning to Martin and myself.

'Oh, yes please,' I piped up. 'I am always ready to listen to erotica which I find most gratifying to my senses.'

Martin nodded his agreement. 'Oh yes, do continue, Andrew, I find all this even more interesting than your Uncle MacGregor's little book on Scottish flora and fauna.'

'But first,' Martin continued, 'I would like to ask both you girls the ages of the youngest and oldest men you have ever fucked. My old friend Professor Shackleton of Cambridge University is undertaking some research in this field and I promised that I would supply him with as much raw data as I could possibly find.'

'Is this the Professor Shackleton who wrote about the meaning of colours in the newspaper recently?' I asked.

'The very same – he is a most learned gentleman and worthy of help in his labours,' said Martin.

'I think that young Leon is my youngest so far,' said Holly. 'How about you, Jenny?'

'Young Geoffrey, the third son of Major Bloodworth was only just a week away from his sixteenth birthday when I first sucked his prick,' I said. 'I don't think I have fucked anyone over thirty five except Doctor David Lezaine, the Belgian specialist in intimate affairs.' (Editor's Note: See *Jenny Everleigh 5: The American Dream*).

Holly mused: 'I once had a lover of fifty six. He really was a game old boy. I refer to the Duke of C– who is a good friend of my Aunt Heather. I was dining with the Duke and to my astonishment I saw his hands slide under the table and come to rest on my thighs. Surely this cannot be so, I thought to myself as one of his hands began to rub insinuatingly between my legs. But there as plain as a pikestaff was a tell-tale bulge between his legs and I decided that such gallantry from a gentleman of his years deserved its reward.

'As we were dining in a private room at Quaglino's, I quickly stripped myself down to the buff and knelt before the Duke to unbutton his straining trousers. His well-veined purple truncheon stood up sturdily as I released it from its confines and I pulled down his trousers until they were round his ankles. I licked his balls until he was fully erect and sank my mouth down over his prick which was now jerking frantically as he grunted with delight. I stopped sucking for a moment to rub my firm breasts over his balding head until he grabbed a tittie and began sucking it furiously. I proceeded to sit on his lap, carefully inserting his pole into my juicy cunney and I bounced gaily up and down. He squeezed my nipples as I cried out that I was about to spend and he pumped a copious amount of white spunk into me as I reached my own peak of pleasure and sent rivulets of juice over the tops of his thighs.'

'How absolutely spiffing! It shows that a good lover can be of any age if he knows how to handle his equipment,' I said, 'but it's Andrew's turn now to tell us of his latest escapades in the boudoir.'

'Very well, ladies, I will not disappoint you but before I forget I wish to ask Martin a question as I recall that last year he was suffering from a condition that I seem to be suffering from at the moment.'

'How can I help you?' enquired the Swedish scientist.

'Well, it's a little bit embarrassing. I was fucking Lady Maureen W– (her husband does not know so I must keep her full name a secret), a couple of weeks ago and I found that I could not ejaculate. My balls seem to go up inside my body and this hurts a little. Is this anything to worry about?'

'Do not be alarmed,' said Martin, 'as I suffered from a very similar complaint last year and I went to see Doctor Roy Stevenson, the world's foremost authority on fucking, and explained my predicament. He told me that the balls draw up inside the body when the man feels cold – and in Sweden, one is cold

71

throughout our long winter. The body naturally protects this delicate mechanism and my body – and yours too – is simply being "over-protective". However, if it happens continually, see a specialist such as Jenny's friend, Doctor Lezaine who will examine you.

'And an occasional failure to spend whilst having sex or when masturbating may be due simply to tiredness or even that your heart really isn't in it! Mind, with you, Andrew, that's a very hard thing to believe. More likely, in your case, you have simply been fucking too much, too often, and you must rest your weary prick.'

'Thank you for your advice,' said Andrew grimly, 'I refuse to even contemplate giving up fucking. Instead I will keep myself in better trim, take a morning constitutional daily and give up rich food and drink.'

'Stop smoking too,' advised Holly, 'it is a foul habit and does you no good whatsoever. Men who smoke are always short of breath which makes them poor lovers as well as to whatever damage smoking does to their hearts and lungs. And I can hardly abide the smell of tobacco on a man's breath, can you, Jenny?'

'I must say that I also dislike it and so do many of my acquaintances feel likewise. Why, my oldest friend Rosie Cox, an aptly-named girl indeed for she loves to have a prick up her cunt more than anything else in the world, refuses to touch the cock of any man who smokes cigarettes or pipes. She does, however, make an exception for those who smoke big cigars.

'I do not take such a definite stand as Rosie, but I must say that any boy who wants to get into my

72

knickers, as the popular vernacular has it, would be well advised to forswear tobacco. I too dislike the odour intensely.'

'I'll bear what you say in mind,' Andrew promised, 'and as far as Martin in concerned, Jenny, you are in luck because he doesn't smoke at all, do you, my Scandinavian friend?

'Anyway,' he continued, 'I shall now tell you of my latest conquest which happened just three nights ago at a soirée at Lady Teasle's home in Green Street. I had been summoned by Lady Teasle to attend as she had persuaded Herr Franzmann, the German tenor now pulling them in at Covent Garden to give a recital of Schubert's lieder.

'I have always found German a tedious language and frankly I would prefer a visit to the music-hall any evening rather than hear some fat fellow belt out these mournful German songs but what could I do? Lady Teasle is one of my mother's oldest friends and you can be sure that my refusal would lead to a stern note going round to the Scott home which in turn would lead to a reduction in the old allowance Mama makes me every quarter. It's hard enough to manage my finances as it is and if I don't pay my tailor, Mr Rabinowitz, the old goat has threatened to take out a writ. Still, that's by the by . . .

'Well, I had dined at the Jim Jam before I arrived and you must believe me when I tell you that I had only consumed about three quarters of a bottle of the Club claret. But when I arrived chez Teasle Lord Denis greeted me in the hall. "Here, old boy, have a glass of this punch. I made it myself, you know, it's the only way I can get through these damned musical evenings my dear lady wife insists on inflicting upon London Society."

'I could hardly refuse so we toasted each other in Lord Denis's punch and I gasped as the fiery liquid hit the back of my throat. "Is that punch, sir?" I spluttered, "there's more than wine and fruit in that concoction I'll be bound."

'"Quite right," grunted Lord Denis, "I've thrown in three bottles of brandy and six bottles of a not very distinguished whisky along with a couple of tumblers of neat gin."

'"Good grief, you will have everyone merry enough," I commented. "Damn right," said Lord Denis with a grim satisfaction, "My manservant, Austin, was groggy after only a couple of swallows. You can take it though, can't you young Andrew? Just like your old Dad, a real chip off the old block. Gad, I remember getting tight with your Papa at the Portuguese Embassy a few years back ... yes, let's have another one and toast your dear Papa. How is he keeping? Your Mama came up to town without him last month."

'"He's well enough, sir," I replied. "He had too much work on the estate to accompany my mother to London which is why he let her go alone." As I did not care to wash our family's dirty linen in public, I omitted to mention the fact that in my opinion my dear Papa was attempting with some success to stick the paternal prick into the juicy pussey of Susie, the cheeky little chambermaid we had just taken into service, especially as I had every intention of following my dear old Dad.

'I walked unsteadily into the drawing room and sat down rather heavily next to a very attractive girl. Herr Franzmann was making the final arrangements with his accompanist, the talented amateur pianist Mr Peter Stockman who is also known amongst the *cognoscenti* as the man with the largest testicles in his home county of Kent. Whether he fucks as well as he plays the piano is open to question but he does have a queue of well-dressed Society women beating a path to his door.'

'Do not speak badly about Society,' advised Holly, 'only people who cannot get into it do that.'

Andrew bowed his apologies and continued his story. 'Well, I composed myself and focused my eyes on the pretty creature sitting next to me. Why it was none other than Belinda Barley, a dear friend of my sister Jane whom I had not seen for at least six months.

'Belinda is a slender, extremely attractive girl who is blessed with extremely large breasts. She was wearing an extremely fetching off the shoulders blue gown and, emboldened by Lord Denis's potent punch, I informed her that she was by far the most pretty female in the room.

'"That is most kind of you, Andrew," she smiled, "but how about my cousin Cecily who is sitting with Cuthbert, her fiancé two rows behind us?"

'I turned my head and looked at Belinda's cousin. She certainly was a dazzlingly pretty girl of about twenty years of age, just a little older than Belinda. She had dark, curly hair which she wore trussed up, though I could imagine it cascading down her white shoulders, and she had large appealing eyes and a wide sensual mouth which when opened showed a set of pearly white even teeth.

'"She really is a beauty," I agreed, "but I still stick to my previous statement!"

'"How gallant," laughed Belinda. "I have an idea, though. Why don't you and I go out before the concert begins. I am sure that Cuthbert and Cecily will follow us. We won't be missed for almost all the chairs are already taken and I can see that there are still some guests in the hall who will want to be seated."

'"What a splendid idea," I said warmly, "come on, then."

'We tiptoe'd our way out and sure enough Cecily and Cuthbert immediately followed us. The hall was now empty except for Lord Denis who was lying on the floor with his head against the wall, sleeping off the effects of his imbibing.

'Belinda made the necessary introductions and then Cecily had the clever idea of taking the tray of drinks and sandwiches on the hall table upstairs to the billiards room. "Capital," said Cuthbert, "I'll take these two bottles of Veuve Cliquot if Andrew could manage the sandwiches and glasses."

'We made our way up to the billiards room and I admired the full size table Lord Denis had installed there. "Such smooth green baize," I commented as we quaffed our glasses of champagne.

'"Indeed it is of the highest quality," said Belinda, her face slightly flushed from the effects of the punch and the champagne. "It is rather warm in here, though, is it not? Cousin Cecily, if you would not mind locking the door, perhaps I would be able to cool myself."

'Cecily locked the door with alacrity as Belinda hoisted herself up to sit on the side of the billiard table. "Do be careful of the baize, Belinda," I said as I knew how proud Lord Denis was of his hand-built table.

'"Well, take my shoes off, Andrew," she commanded and I helped the lovely girl to do so. Cecily now jumped up besides Belinda and said: "You are right, darling Bee, it is very warm in here. Cuthbert, take off my shoes as well if you please."

'He too obeyed the command with a small grin but his jaw dropped and his eyebrows shot up when he saw his pretty fiancée undo the buttons on Belinda's silk blouse and my face too must have been a real study when Belinda returned the compliment!

'The girls carefully folded their blouses and put them down carefully on the green baize. Then they unhinged their suspenders and peeled off their stockings and giggling away they proceeded to unbutton their skirts and helped each other to pull off their slips so that all they were wearing were flimsy little cream silk knickers.

'"You too buy your knickers at Madame Silviano's?" giggled Belinda, stroking her magnificently large, creamy breasts that were tipped with delightfully round aureoles and exquisitely fashioned nipples.

'"Yes, I am a regular patron," replied the equally delicious Cecily whose own breasts, though not Belinda's equal in size, jutted out proudly and were capped by two red stalked strawberry nipples that simply ached to be sucked.

'One look at Cuthbert's trousers showed that like myself, his prick was growing stiffer by the second and my own tool bulged even more uncomfortably when Belinda said: "Help us off with our knickers, boys, if you don't mind." They raised their bottoms invitingly as I took hold of Belinda's and Cuthbert took hold of Cecily's and pulled them down to and over their well-shaped ankles. The girls gaily kicked them off and both Cuthbert and I began to undress – we needed no further words of direction from the girls as we struggled with buttons, shoelaces and cuff-links.

'You may well imagine that my cock was at action

stations and raring to sink into Belinda's juicy pussey, but regretfully, he had to wait, for to my suprise the two girls began to embrace and fell backwards onto the table. Their limbs entwined but I could see that Cecily was taking the masculine role in the proceedings as she worked Belinda's large, stalked-up nipples between her thumb and forefinger.

'I relaxed somewhat and enjoyed the two girls' party piece and watched with fascination as Cecily's left hand continued to toy with Belinda's breast while her right hand slid down her belly and then onto her thick, bushy pubic mound. I leaned forward to see Cecily's forefinger disappear between Belinda's pussey lips and the young tribades exchanged voluptuous kisses until Cecily broke away to nuzzle Belinda's right tittie, drawing it deep inside her eager mouth.

'I could see that Cecily now had two fingers sliding in and out of Belinda's cunt, moving them so swiftly that they were almost vibrating. Her thumb rapidly skated back and forth over Belinda's swollen clitty which I could see protruding between her pussey lips. Belinda then arched her back, squirming with pleasure as she jerked into a delightful orgasm.

'Now it was Belinda's turn to repay her pretty cousin who turned her back on Belinda, grinding her shapely bum-cheeks on Belinda's dripping pussey. Belinda pushed her hips forward and the two rocked in rhythm as Belinda caressed Cecily's titties from behind, flicking the red nipples up to little peaks of pulsating red stalks. Then she pulled her hand down to attack her cunney, slipping her hands in and out until Cecily was fairly shaking with passionate desire.

'Belinda pulled Cecily down on her back and then climbed directly on top of her so that they were now glued together with their breasts and cunnies mashed together. "Now, Cecily," gasped Belinda, "I am going to put my own stiff little cunney between your cunney lips. Look, I am pushing it in, can you feel it?"

'"Yes, yes, yes," shrieked Cecily, "more, more, more!" So Belinda pushed forward as hard as she could but the sight of these two tribades proved too much for Cuthbert who leaped up on the table, rolled the two girls on their sides so that their bare bottoms were open to view, and taking his meaty prick in his hand, attempted to force a passage between Cecily's magnificent buttocks.

'"Ah, how splendid!" panted Cecily, "I would love your cock up my arse, Cuthbert but for heaven's sake spread some pomade on it first." To their immense joy, I happened to note a tin of cream on a side table and I said: "Hold on a moment, I will anoint Cuthbert's cock for you."

'I too was now on the table and kneeling down. I opened the tin and applied a liberal smearing of pomade to Cuthbert's throbbing cock, coating the hot shaft with a layer of thin grease which excited him so much that he nearly spent on my hand. Such a disaster was fortunately avoided and I again aided the happy couple by parting Cecily's bum-cheeks to reveal her wrinkled little arse-hole and I placed the smooth purplish dome of Cuthbert's cock to its edge.

'Cuthbert expertly inserted the tip of his prick, which was well-sized for a bottom-fuck being of only medium girth but of an especial length, into the sweet girl's bum and the threesome now writhed in new paroxyms of pleasure.

'"Come on, Andrew, isn't my cunt good enough for you?" called out Belinda, opening her legs a trifle to tickle Cecily's cunney with her hand.

'I needed no further urging and I knelt my way across to take up position behind the gorgeous wench. She lifted her bottom slightly to effect an easy lodgement for my pulsating prick which slid into her dripping love-crack from behind with the utmost ease. What bliss! What absolute feelings of total abandon seeped through my body as I pumped my trusty tool in and out of her squelchy cunney as Belinda continued to frig Cecily's cunt whilst Cuthbert fucked her bottom and I fucked Belinda's cunt giving the girls the benefit of a double helping of delight. It was all so exciting that Cuthbert and I both spent fairly quickly and I could almost feel my balls lighten as I squirted jet after jet of frothy white jism into Belinda's sopping cunney. The girls too had climbed the summits of the mountains of love and we all sank back on the table quite sated by this novel experience.

'"My God! Look how our juices have stained the baize!" said Belinda anxiously. "I fear that even Lady Jemima Gaffney's elixir won't be able to clean it up."

'"Not to worry," said Cuthbert cheerfully, "I have loads of money and I will simply arrange for an artisan to come round here tomorrow morning and measure up for a new covering. The table is of standard size and it won't take too long to do. Why, Lord Denis is in no fit state to play tonight and even if he wants a game tomorrow evening, by then the table will look as good as new."

'"How wonderfully clever of you, Cuthbert," said Cecily, "I think you deserve to have your cock kissed for that, don't you agree, Belinda?"

'"Indeed I do," said Belinda warmly, "on the condition that you allow me to share the sucking."

'"Of course," said Cecily sweetly, "I wouldn't dream of not keeping it in the family."

'The girls giggled and Belinda took hold of Cuthbert's limp shaft, rubbing it vigorously until her soft touch performed the usual magical effect of swelling up the affair until it stood stiffly to attention. Belinda jammed his foreskin down and exposed the smooth, velvety dome of his knob and motioned to Cecily that she should have the joy of the first suck of the succulent sweetmeat. She sucked deeply, letting the dome slide against her cheek whilst her lips smacked noisily as she lubricated Cuthbert's shaft. She then grasped the throbbing pole and began to lick it up and down whilst Belinda opened her mouth and popped in the glistening knob which she now sucked with uninhibited pleasure, lapping and nibbling at the uncapped dome which sent Cuthbert into the realms of sheer ecstasy.

'We dressed ourselves rapidly and as we did so Belinda mused: "It suddenly strikes me that this evening is three years to the very evening of my first fuck."

'"Gracious, what a memory," I said. "Allow me to offer my congratulations."

'"It is also," she continued blithely, "the third anniversary of my second fuck and indeed my third and forth."

'"Goodness me, that sounds most exciting but also exceedingly hectic for a young gel," said Cuthbert, twirling his luxuriant moustache.

'"Not really, Cuthbert," smiled Belinda. "One evening; four fucks. All one after the other with extended intervals between the third and fourth."

'"You certainly started with a bang," said Cecily.

'"Don't be coarse," said Belinda, pretending to be cross, "or I shall not tell you about it."

'"Oh, that would be too cruel," answered Cecily. "You know full well how we all love to hear of such things. You simply must tell us every last detail. See, the boys' cocks can clearly be seen outlined against their trousers and as for me, just give me your hand a moment." And so saying, she took Belinda's hand and placed it between her legs, squeezing her thighs tightly together.

'"I see that I shall have to confess how I lost my virginity," sighed Belinda. "I wish I had not remembered the anniversary now although I suppose we have nothing better to do as the concert won't finish for at least an hour and we can hardly re-enter the room to hear Herr Franzmann even if we wished to do so."

'"Precisely so," I said, "and we cannot very well go downstairs in case Lord Denis wakes up. Therefore I suggest we make ourselves comfortable and you can tell us how you lost your virginity. If there is time, I shall follow you with my own first experience in *l'arte de faire l'amour*."'

I looked out of the window and noticed that we were now slowly moving again. 'We will certainly have time to hear how Belinda's pussey was first pierced by the arrow of love,' I remarked. 'But the tale of your own first plunging your prick inside a nice wet pussey will have to wait until the return journey.'

I blushed as the words left my lips as I realised that I had been uncommonly forthright in my blunt comments. Dear Holly must have sensed my embarrassed confusion for she said: 'Well put, Jenny, I am sure the boys appreciate your lack of reserve and use of pithy phrases. But don't do it again – at least until we are on our way home for you will make my damp pussey itch with desire that will have to remain unslaked until this afternoon at the very earliest!'

Just as she uttered these words the train came to a sudden, juddering halt. 'Oh dear,' said Sir Andrew, 'more trouble on the line, I'll be bound. Shall I continue or would someone else take on the story-teller's role as my throat is somewhat parched!'

'It's your turn, Jenny,' continued Sir Andrew thoughtfully, 'I would suggest that if you have no objection you tell us of the first time you enjoyed the delicious sensation of a hot prick entering your damp cunney.'

The suggestion was not without merit so I nodded my head and said: 'First love can be idyllic or it can be unmitigated disaster. I was fortunate to have a loving tutor who took the time and trouble to cater for my every need to make my first act of sexual union a delicious experience for us both.

'I had just celebrated my seventeenth birthday and I was still in possession of my maidenhead – technically I was still a virgin although my hymen had been subjected to many strains. I should recount what had happened to me during the four years I spent at Miss Bradshaw's Academy for Young Ladies in Dorset where two hundred and seventy girls, deprived of any contact whatsoever with the opposite sex, naturally developed many inter-feminine friend-ships of an intimate nature.

'Many were the intense conversations conducted on staircases or in quiet corners and many were the sly touches, the gentle pressures of hands on hands that ached for an answering response. Many an arm was slipped casually around my slim waist in the expectation of a quick smile and an equally swift hip-to-hip rub as a signal that other and greater intimacies might be enjoyed in the near future.

'My own favourite bedmate was a French girl, Antoinette de Bergerac, a beautiful dark girl from near Cannes in the South of France. She had a plump figure, large sensuous eyes and flesh as smooth and polished as ivory. She seemed to take a great fancy to me and as we shared a small room together she kissed and hugged me so lovingly that I felt slightly confused at first as she took such liberties with me. I well remember the night that she first placed her soft hands on the most private parts of my person, and how her searching gropings made me all atremble.

'She covered my mouth with hers and kissed me passionately, unbuttoning my nightdress until I could slip my arms out of the garment. She cupped my firm breasts and rubbed my titties against the palms of her hands, swelling up the little stalks to a fine erection.

'"Off with your chemise, Jenny," she smiled, "and I too will take off my chemise de nuit." She stood up and surveyed her beautiful naked figure in the large cheval glass. "Come and stand next to me, Jenny," she called and I got out of bed and stood next to Antoinette who hugged me and patted my light haired pussey.

'"Let us compare our pussies," she continued, "I do love your pouting little crack, Jenny, what a fine contrast we make, your light blonde hair and my black curly moss. Come back into bed and I will frig you until your pussey is all nice and juicy."

'We jumped back into bed and she covered me in

kisses before inserting her finger into my dampening cunney. "Oooh, that's nice, Antoinette, oooh, I love this game. Tickle me more with your fingers," I breathed. "With pleasure, Jenny," she replied, renewing her frigging of my pussey which sent a most luscious longing sensation all over me and I begged her to shove her fingers right up. "Oh! Oh! How delightful! Further! Harder!" I called out and almost fainted with delight as she brought down the first warm, creamy spend not brought on by my own squeezing of my thighs and tickling of my own cunney.

'Next night we repeated our amusements with the lovely girl laying on top of me with my tongue in her mouth as she frigged me to orgasm. How lovely it was, I can hardly express my raptures and movements as I spent with extraordinary profusion into her busy hand.

'My cunney had been severely tested by this little exercise and indeed I had been forced to take a small towel to my pussey which was sopping wet from the mixture of my spendings and some sanguine pearls which at first worried me until Antoinette reassured me that there was nothing to concern myself with as the blood came only from the first breaking of the hymen.

'Antoinette now stood again in front of the cheval mirror, surveying herself at full length. What magnificent swelling breasts she possessed and what a clear whiteness of belly set off by the dark forest of curly hair through which I could perceive the outline of her glistening slit. A self-satisfied smile parted her cherry lips and displayed the sparkling pearls of teeth as she patted the marble skin of her belly. Then she playfully parted the lips of her cunt and examined it closely in the glass. The titillation of her fingers brought a blush to her cheek and she moved her fingers in and out of her pussey almost lazily, gently frigging herself, moving her fingers slowly in and out between the vermilion lips of love.

'I was quite fired by her uninhibited behaviour and began to frig my own pussey as Antoinette said: "Dear Jenny, I will leave you for a while but I wish to have a nice, warm bath." She slipped on a robe and I heard her close the door and pad quietly down the corridor. I stayed there alone, lying nude on the bed, with my eyes closed gently thinking of the pretty girl as my hands snaked down towards my cunney. But to my horror I heard a stifled cough and opening my eyes in a flash I saw that I was not alone!

'Standing in front of me was young Walter Godfrey, the second son of the school secretary and administrator. My first thought was to grab the eiderdown and cover my naked charms. I was startled but not afraid as Walter, who was eighteen months older than me and was staying with his parents during the University vacation, had obtained the last waltz on my card at the school Spring Ball. And afterwards we had strolled down to Nolan's Fields where we had kissed amorously and I had let Walter cup his hands around my breasts and I had stroked the enormous bulge between his legs but I had resisted his attempts to put his hand under my skirt even though I did enjoy his pressing down on my burning pussey through the silk material of my dress. We went for walks a good few times after that and usually ended up kissing and cuddling though I would not let the dear boy take any further liberties than those I have already described.

'"Walter, you naughty boy to frighten me so!" I scolded the handsome young scoundrel.

'"You must forgive the intrusion, Jenny," he blurted out, "but in all honesty I had only intended to pop into your room to offer you the loan of this excellent book, Human Procreation Explained For Boys and Girls by the celebrated Doctor Roy Stevenson, the well-known authority on *les affaires d'amour*. I thought that if you would read it, our relationship could progress further than it has now and I, er, I ..." and his voice trailed off as he could see my eyes were riveted to the huge bulge between his legs.

'I could have told him that I was well acquainted with Doctor Stevenson's marvellous little volume (I dined with Doctor Stevenson at the Pokinghams a few nights ago, by the by) but all my attention was drawn to that curiously exciting bulge between Walter's legs.

'Oh, but he was a handsome lad, I remember the first time that I saw him at a concert his uncle, Sir Louis Baum, had arranged for the girls of Miss Bradshaw's Academy and the boys of Professor Febeson's School for Young Gentlemen situated just six miles away. The very moment he walked into the room my heart began pounding. Perhaps it was the set of his muscular shoulders or the clearness of his deep blue eyes that raked the gathering of girls with a predatory gaze as he cut through the crowd with the cool glide of a panther stalking its prey.

'"Jenny, do you want to see what the sight of your gorgeous bare breasts and heavenly little cunt has done to me?" he burst out.

'"I rather think I do," I replied, "for surely as you have glimpsed my naked charms it would be fitting for me to see yours." The scamp needed no further bidding and he shucked off his clothes in a time almost quicker than I can relate this lewd tale, he stood naked in front of me. Walter was a real Adonis with a broad chest, narrow waist and fine long legs but what attracted my fullest attention was his beautiful cock which was standing stiffly up to his belly button. I motioned him to come forward and I threw off the eiderdown and reached out to grab this red-headed monster which I had now seen for the first time in all its naked glory.

'I had never taken a prick in my mouth before, but my lips were drawn as if by an invisible magnet to the mushroom dome of Walter's lovely cock. I kissed the smooth, hot head and thoroughly wet the top and opening my mouth, took the knob in and sucked around the throbbing sweetmeat. Ah, it tasted so masculine, with a salty tang that I closed my lips around it as tightly as possible and worked on the tip with my tongue, easing my lips forward to take in more of the shaft. Young Walter had suffered from a tight foreskin when he was a small child and had undergone a minor operation to remove the offending appendage so I was able to rub his shaft up and down without hindrance, an act which I undertook with uninhibited voluptuousness.

'I circled the base of his great tool and he pushed my head down until I could take no more of his huge stalk. In fact, I tried to take too much of his cock into my mouth and I almost choked in doing so. "Don't worry, Jenny," whispered Walter, "let me rub your titties whilst you play with my prick."

'He began to flick at my hard little nipples, exciting me even more as my fingers slid over his cock and balls. With both hands I cupped his hairy balls and massaged them gently, lifting and separating each one. Then I grabbed his prick with both hands, one on top of the other and started a sliding action that drove poor Walter into a frenzy. I pumped and jerked his shaft so well that his prick began to jerk uncontrollably in my hands and then with a loud moan he squirted out jets of white semen into my hands.

'I was fascinated by his spending but being a young man in his prime, Walter did not have to rest before continuing the joust. He gave his cock a quick little rub and it was back to its full height. He pulled me to him and kissed me deeply, his tongue parting my lips and twisting in my mouth. His strong hands were now on my bum-cheeks, pulling them apart and he pushed a single finger into my tight little bum-hole which both hurt and excited me at the same time. I felt his cock stiffly beating against my tummy as we rolled onto the bed and Walter's hands found my crack immediately, and the dear boy slid his long, tapering fingers inside my damp slit, causing me to wriggle and twist in his embrace.

'He stroked my hair and pulled my face to his, pushing his tongue down my throat as he continued the cunt-fingering, and then he brought the tip of his cock to my cunney-lips. He jiggled his knob around just inserting the very tip and then pushed forward gently just an inch or so until meeting little or no resistance he thrust forward fully and I felt the last remains of virginal barrier crumble before the onslaught of his fierce prick. There was only a slight discomfort which changed to a delicious sensation as his cock slicked through my sopping cunt, in and out, in and out as Walter thoughtfully pulled my lips open with his hand to ease the passage of his prick.

'"Is this real fucking, Walter?" I gasped as his balls banged against my bum.

'"Well, it's certainly not croquet," he replied

89

wittily, "and indeed it is more fun than croquet, cricket, footer and all the other games put together. Yes, this is fucking, Jenny Everleigh. I am fucking your gorgeous cunt with my thick prick. How do you like it?"

'"Oh, very much, very much," I breathlessly answered, "I do so agree with you, Walter, that fucking is the finest sport of all."

'This reply set Walter off again. He had tried to keep his strokes nice and slow but now he changed up a gear, really banging his cock into me at a rate of knots, his balls slopping against my bottom with each fierce attack as he thrust into my ripe young pussey with all the energy he could muster.

'I was now also past the point of no return and I felt another awesome climax welling up inside me. I shuddered as Walter too began to spend, flooding me with hot, creamy spunk as my own juices flowed freely, mingling with his love-juices as with an immense cry of joy, I achieved my first full ascent of the mountain of joy.'

I paused for breath and Martin, whose lap now bulged with a fearsome looking erection that threatened to burst through his trousers, said huskily: 'That is one of the most exciting anecdotes I have ever heard. You have made my prick very excited . . .'

'Indeed you have, Jenny,' laughed Sir Andrew, 'I think it only fair that you grant Martin some relief. There isn't time for a real fuck before Handcross but another kind of Hand, perhaps . . .'

His request was a fair one and could not go unheeded, I thought, so I unbuttoned Martin's straining trousers and out popped his proudly erect cock. To my surprise, his cock also lacked a foreskin and I commented on this unusual fact but Martin assured me that circumcision (as the removal of the foreskin is called) is very popular amongst many upper class people in Scandinavia.

'I hope that you do not find my cock too strange?' enquired Martin anxiously.

'Oh, no, not in the slightest. I am quite used to circumcised cocks as I have been fucked by several Hebrew gentlemen and as you know the Jews and the Mohammedans take off the foreskin almost immediately after birth. In fact, I think that a circumcised cock has a lot to commend it,' I said, grasping Martin's not inconsiderable tool with both my hands and rubbing it up and down in a slow, regular rhythm.

'Hurry up, Jenny,' called out Holly, 'we are almost at the station.'

'I'm going as fast as I can,' I replied. 'Why not give me a hand?'

The pretty girl said: 'I'll give you my lips instead,' and bending her head down she licked all round the knob of Martin's cock. This new delight combined with my own ministrations had the required effect and Martin's prick exploded into action with a jet of frothy spunk shooting out of his knob. Unfortunately Holly was too slow in removing her head and a wad of white jism hit her in the eye whilst the remainder of his emission finished up all over his navy blue trousers.

'Don't worry,' advised Sir Andrew, 'we will stop off at the village store for a bottle of Doctor Malcolm Campbell's stain remover. It is highly efficacious even for spunk stains.'

I remembered that Connor, my butler who I had fucked the week before had told me of this preparation but since then I had also been informed of Lady Gaffney's wonderful mixture.

'I understand that Lady Jemima Gaffney also has a special concoction that is extremely useful in such circumstances,' I said.

'Oh yes,' said Holly brightly, 'but you can't buy it over the counter like Doctor Campbell's – and incidentally, I use Lady Gaffney's mixture as an excellent cure for constipation if my dogs are having problems. You may care to note this down for future reference.'

The train pulled into the little station and we climbed out and straight into the awaiting carriage that took us to Nymans Gardens. I am too tired, diary, to recount the interesting time we spent there except to record that a most enjoyable time was had by all – especially perhaps by Martin and myself as I sucked off the dear lad underneath a rather phallic looking tree the shape of which reminded me of his nice smooth prick. The journey back to London was uneventful but my lovely day was spoiled somewhat by a slight headache before supper. So I excused myself from the party which was going to dine at the Jim Jam before going to the Alhambra music hall to see the eccentric comedian Mr Billy Coote and instead retired to bed early to begin writing up this narrative to record for posterity this voluptuous day.


*30 September 1889*
As you are well aware, dearest diary, yesterday was supposed to have been spent recovering from my trip to Nymans Gardens but my morning rest was disturbed (if that is the correct word for in truth I was delighted to see him) by a most unexpected visitor.

When Connor announced that there was a Mister Donne in the hall asking whether I was at home I did not think for a moment that it could be my old friend from America, Ronnie Donne, the randiest dentist in the entire New World! I wondered indeed who this strange gentleman could be and I was minded indeed to send the man away without seeing him as I rarely entertain any visitors without prior appointments.

Fortunately, my curiosity won over any lingering doubts and I told Connor to show in the gentleman. When he returned with the unknown guest I was amazed to see that the stranger was none other than dear Ronnie.

'Jenny!' he cried out, 'Jenny Everleigh, how marvellous to see your pretty face again!'

'Dearest Ronnie, it is delightful to see *you* again. What a wonderful surprise! I had no idea it was you when Connor told me that a strange gentleman was waiting to see me. Why didn't you give me your card?'

'Oh, I wanted to surprise you, my little English rose. Tell me all the news – are you keeping well?'

We exchanged pleasantries and all the news and gossip about mutual friends on both sides of the Atlantic Ocean. I was delighted to hear that Ronnie's friend David Juckson was due to arrive from New York next week with the avowed intention of opening an American style restaurant in London.

Connor brought in morning coffee and I asked Ronnie how long he would be staying in London. 'About another two weeks, I guess,' he said, 'I'm staying at the Jim Jam in Great Windmill Street. I arrived three nights ago but I have been extremely busy with business meetings so I thought I would first wrap up all these tiresome affairs before calling upon you.'

'What business affairs can an American dentist have in London?' I wondered.

'Ah, you see, I have patented a new method of painlessly extracting teeth and hope to follow this up with an equally painless way of making your high-class lords and ladies extract gold sovereigns from their banks!' laughed Ronnie, his blue eyes twinkling in the fashion that first led me to wish his huge cock in my pussey when I visited his surgery back in New York City.

Ronnie Donne is one of my favourite men. He is in his mid-forties, not too tall but blessed with a powerful, stocky figure, a handsome rugged face and as I found out soon after meeting him, is possessed of a very, very fine cock which he uses to great effect.

'Do you know, Jenny, I must be getting old,' said Ronnie, 'for I feel so tired even at this early hour.'

'I hope you are not ill,' I said.

'No, no, my sweet. I think I have simply taken too much exercise – and not the indoor exercises which I prefer! I met a chap in the Jim Jam last night, a writer guy named Rodney Burbeck who was extolling the virtues of bicycling to me.

'I've ridden a bicycle before now but not for long journeys so I readily agreed when Rodney proposed that we ask the club secretary to hire us two machines so that we could go out for a spin.

'We dined lightly on Dover sole and then we took a slow ride through the traffic to Hyde Park Corner and went into the park to be free of the many vehicles that blocked Piccadilly and the surrounding streets.

'Now we were free to ride at our own speed and the darkness gave us an involuntary thrill for our eyes were still blinded by the dazzling lights of Mayfair. It's great fun, Jenny, I do assure you, riding a bicycle at night in the near dark. When your eyes have become somewhat accustomed to the dimness they wander to the ground and you can make out the luminous circle cast by your lamp.

'After running into the side of the road a few times more or less gently, your eyes become used to the darkness and you gradually recover your self-confidence. Anyhow, Rodney Burbeck and I covered at least six miles before cycling back to the Club where we both had a quick whisky and soda before retiring to bed around half past eleven o'clock.'

'A somewhat exhausting evening but you should surely have made a full recovery by now,' I said.

'You are absolutely right,' he admitted, 'but as I was about to retire there was a knock on the door and a sweet young voice called out: "Mr Donne, it's Marsha the maid here. May I turn down the covers for you?"

'"Of course," I said, "come right in." I had just taken a bath but I had a long bath-towel draped round my middle so there would be no embarrassment caused to either me or my visitor. Marsha came in and I have to admit, Jenny, that she was a stunner. I had spoken briefly to her earlier in the day and had ascertained that she was nineteen years old and came from Camberwell in South London. Now I don't know how we came to talking of intimate matters –'

'Not much you don't, Ronnie, don't fool me!' I laughed.

He returned my laugh and continued: 'O K Jenny,

fair enough but anyhow it turned out that this gorgeous girl had taken up naturism as a hobby. You know what naturism is, Jenny?'

'No, I don't think I have heard the term before.'

'No? Then I will explain it to you. Naturism is the practice of going about without any clothes on. Naturists hold that the sunlight is not harmful to the body as we believe but in fact is highly beneficial and should reach even our most tender private parts.'

'Don't tell me that this girl converted you to naturism in just a couple of minutes!'

'Oh, no. But Marsha was something of an exhibitionist and she insisted on telling me what had happened to her that very afternoon whilst she turned down my bed. She said: "I do enjoy being a naturist. Why, this afternoon when the weather was at its finest, I went up to the roof of the Club and took off all my clothes. I lay face down on a blanket I had brought up the ladder with me and exposed my bottom cheeks to the bright sunlight.

'"Then I heard a loud hammering from the building next door. I turned over and saw four young men working on the roof of Louis Rabinowitz's casino next door. They were staring open-mouthed at my exposed large breasts and the dark tufts of hair that covered my cunt. This really excited me and made my blood boil so I decided to put on a little cabaret show for them. I started to massage my large titties, gently squeezing the nipples and really turning myself on. I became hornier and hornier and began to finger fuck myself, slipping my fingers in and out of my crack until I was writhing away with great spasms of pleasure rippling through my body.

'"One of the men was so carried away that he jumped the four feet gap between the two roofs to obtain a bird's eye view and as he approached I saw it was young Michael Seagull, a curiously named but handsome young devil employed by old Rabinowitz for general labouring duties. I was now so far gone that I said: "Come on Michael, is your cock big enough to fuck my hot cunney?"

'"He undid his belt, pulled down his trousers and underpants to expose a fully erect thick cock that would have looked big on any man let alone a mere youth of seventeen. He climbed between my legs and sank this huge cock deep inside my waiting cunney. It was to be a quick fuck as we were both perhaps over-excited but after we had both spent I went down and took Michael's cock between my lips and eagerly sucked his thick pole. He responded by burying his face in my dark muff and nibbled happily on my clitty.

'"At last we rolled apart, absolutely exhausted to the applause of Michael's mates. They had been so taken with watching our fucking that they had all unbuttoned their trousers and were playing with their cocks shooting white fountains of sperm into the gap between the roofs sending a unique kind of rain upon any unsuspecting passer-by down in the alley which separated the two buildings!"'

Ronnie paused for breath and then continued: 'I don't know whether the saucy young minx deliberately meant to excite me but of course by the time she finished this most erotic adventure, my prick was swelling up to its full height and pushing out the soft folds of the towel that was draped around me.'

'"Oh my," she said, "You look most uncomfortable, shall I give you some relief?"

'–"I wish you would!" I exclaimed, and to my joy the gorgeous girl pulled down the towel that was hanging precariously around me so that I stood naked in front of her.

'"That's a nice cock, sir," she said, "let me see what I can do for it."

'She knelt down and shrugged off her apron and blouse so that her beautiful breasts were fully uncovered and she took hold of my throbbing cock and placed it between the cleft of her strong, firm breasts. She put her face down and licked the knob for a little while before she muttered: "Ah, my blood is on fire, I must have that delectable prick in my cunt!"

'I lay her down on my bed as she wriggled out of her skirt and lay there naked. I lay on top of her and after the exchange of burning kisses in which our tongues were almost down each others' throats, I slid down her body slowly, caressing her wonderful bum-cheeks with my hands and kissing her horned up strawberry nipples that hardened under my nibbling. I slid all the way down until my lips were mere inches away from her reddish haired pussey. Instinctively she opened her legs to make the swollen wet pussey lips and already visible little clitty more easily accessible to me. My tongue moved, delving, probing, sliding from the top of her crack to her cunney-hole, my tongue lapping up the fragrant cunt-juice that flowed freely from her.

'I stiffened the tip of my tongue and began to lick the soft, puffed inner lips. I eagerly inhaled the aroma that arose from her and I thrust forcefully with my tongue, making her moan in ecstacy as it pushed into her love-channel which was so warm, wet, and deeply inviting.

'Her hips were gyrating wildly as I stroked my tongue in and out of her. I licked her rhythmically up and down, feeling the swollen flesh pulsing in eager response and her clitty grew harder each time my tongue flicked across it, jerking and rising up to meet the laps of my tongue. I moved my head up to concentrate on her clitty and I adored the way it moved and grew as I concentrated all my attentions upon it. Her clitty grew even harder as I tickled it with my tongue like a miniature prick that stiffened perceptibly by my stimulation. I continued to tease her clitty, driving her wild with slow, firm strokes alternating with light quick jabs until she screamed out: "Fuck me, please fuck me, I want your big cock inside my pussey!"

'Being a gentleman, I gave her pussey a final *au revoir* kiss and turned her over to fuck her doggie-style from behind. This appealed to the exquisite young miss, for she stuck up her rounded bottom cheeks in the air and reached back to fondle my balls and feel my throbbing cock as I pushed my shaft into her welcoming, drenched cunney.

'Holding on to her delicious bum cheeks I began pounding in and out of her cunt with long, deep strokes. She was squealing delightedly and screamed out: "Now! Now! Shoot all your spunk up my pussey!" I was ready to oblige as I could already feel the sperm boiling up inside my balls. I held out for as long as I could and then with a long, loud groan I emptied my powerful jets of frothy spunk into her. She was tearing at the sheets and moaning into the pillows as she enjoyed her own peak of pleasure. Jenny, she was a really grade-A fuck.'

'Was she really?' I said a little coldly.

'Almost as good as you,' added Ronnie hastily. 'We licked and lapped, fucked and sucked each other all night – almost till dawn, which is why I am now so tired.'

'So you thought you could have a nice rest here, I suppose, you cheeky boy!'

'Aw, Jenny, don't be mad. You can't have expected my cock to remain out of a pussey since we last enjoyed a roll in the hay.'

'Of course I had not expected you to remain celibate. Nor indeed have I refrained from enjoying the pleasures of the flesh. But to come here after fucking all night, Ronnie, is a little much, don't you think?'

'I suppose you are right,' admitted the handsome dentist, 'but you asked me why I was so tired and I decided to tell you the truth. Please forgive me, Jenny.'

'Very well, my sweet,' I said, 'it is as well for you that I have such a forgiving nature but I will excuse you this time upon payment of a forfeit.'

'That's fine with me, Jenny. But what will this forfeit be?'

'I'll think about that for a moment.' I said seriously although you know full well, dearest diary that I always knew what I had in mind for Ronnie's forfeit!

'O K,' he said, visibly brightening up. 'Whilst you think of one, let me tell you the funny story I heard from Bernardo Rubeno, the Mexican musician you met in Washington [Editor's Note: See *The Intimate Memoir of Jenny Everleigh 5: The American Dream*] which I suppose is germane to this situation.

'Father Murphy is sitting in the confessional when in rushes Abie Goldberg who says: "Father, Father, I must tell you something. I was walking by your Church just now when this beautiful girl suddenly appears and putting her hand on my cock, begins to rub it until it is bursting out of its confiness. She unbottoned my trousers and took it out and sucked me off. I shot a copious emission of spunk into her mouth which she swallowed and then she sucked me off again and I jetted another wodge of spunk inside her mouth which she greedily swallowed. And I'm sixty six years old!"

'"My son, my son," said the shocked priest. "What are you telling me all this for? You're not even a Catholic."

'"Sorry Father," said Abie, "I just had to tell somebody!"'

I roared with laughter and any anger I felt at hearing about Ronnie's naughty escapade the previous night melted as we cuddled up together on the couch. 'Let's go upstairs,' I whispered. 'Connor the butler has a nasty habit of peering through the keyhole and I don't want him to see us fuck as I always perform best alone or with a specially invited audience.'

'Very true, very true,' agreed Ronnie as we looked out of the door into the hall and finding the coast clear we ran quickly up the stairs into my bedroom. We stripped off our clothes and then we were rolling around naked on my bed, our limbs entwined as I thrilled to the feel of his hard cock up against my stomach.

His fingers lightly caressed my cunney, causing the muscles of my cunt to spasm with pleasure. He felt that I was enjoying myself as he laughed softly and gently stroked the lips of my cunt, playing gently with my fluffy, blonde pussey hair. I pushed my crotch against his hand to increase the pleasure and in response he rubbed a bit harder.

'Oooh,' I gasped as the fire between my legs became hotter and hotter. Ronnie slipped one, then two fingers inside my wet crack, his long fingers groping deep inside me, finding that incredibly sensitive spot at the bottom of my honeypot. I shuddered with desire and started to moan so loudly that he stopped for a moment and looked up anxiously. 'Don't worry,' I whispered. 'The door is locked and Connor is the soul of discretion especially if you cross his palm with silver before you leave!'

With a smile, Ronnie continued to pleasure my pussey, stroking me and stroking me until I thought I would go insane with unslaked desire. I began to whimper uncontrollably as he found my erect little clitty and he began to finger fuck me, using his thumb to massage my clit. My hips were jerking, madly, wildly as I pushed against his hand as my legs spread wide, my thighs gleaming with the juices as I came in a sudden release, clamping my thighs together around his hand as I hugged him with gratitude.

Ah, what bliss lying sated on the rumpled sheets with my lover in my arms. After we had regained our composure, we again rode the wind, Ronnie proving the adage that a hard man is good to find. He was able, alas, to only fuck me twice more before even all my coaxing with my mouth and lips was unable to raise his cock from its exhausted limpness. We girls can fuck far longer than boys, diary, a fact that I have previously noted in your pages. Our cunnies *do* dry up but it only takes a little cream and a very short rest and we are again ready for action. Would that our men were so able to continue jousting so soon after spending!

**END OF PART ONE**

# PART TWO

# A HUNTING WE WILL GO

A further extract from the Intimate Memoir of
Dame Jenny Everleigh

## Preface

This extract from Jenny Everleigh's diaries is dated
a year later than the previous pages. Readers may
care to know that Jenny enjoyed a long liaison with
Ronald Donne, the American dentist who took
Jenny back with him to New York where she stayed
until January before going out to California. She
recorded her experiences in San Francisco, where,
if her diaries are to be believed, the city was
renowned not like today for its gay community, but
for an especially rumbustuous heterosexual reputation.

Jenny came back to London in May 1890 and
tried to resume her friendship with her old friend
Captain Johnny Oaklands. Alas, the magic had left
the relationship and the once strong attachment now
broke up – but it was, as she records, an amicable
parting of the ways.

An inveterate traveller, Jenny accepted an invitation to stay at the castle of Count Gewirtz in Galicia
but again, although the Count was on the point of

proposal, she decided not to stay and returned home in early July.

Her diaries show her to be at somewhat of a loose end until an invitation comes through to join a party up in Scotland for the beginning of the hunting season on 12 August. Although not attracted by the sight of people killing animals purely for pleasure, Jenny was bored with the London scene and so she gratefully accepted the invitation. An extra cause of excitement for her was the promised appearance of the Prince of Wales who, although married to the beautiful Princess Alexandra from Denmark, was already in his prime as a ladies' man. HRH was known only to favour married ladies like Mrs Keppel in an attempt to avoid scandal but sometimes the spirit was willing but the flesh was even more willing, as the uninhibited Jenny Everleigh might have said.

Tim Nayland

*10 August 1890*

At last! The glorious twelfth was nearly upon us! A whole month of sport stretched enticingly in front of us – or rather, for the gentlemen of the party, who had busied themselves in the previous week with almost daily visits to their gunsmiths. For myself, I had sport of a very different nature in mind.

We assembled at King's Cross station, at nine-thirty of the evening of the tenth. Sir Horace, a man who despised haste of any kind, had insisted we be in residence at his Speyside estate in advance of the great day. 'I must be out with the ghillies at once!' he exclaimed. 'How else am I to see how the shooting will go?'

104

The platform seethed with steam and bustle. As a director of the railway company, Sir Horace had secured a sleeping carriage for our exclusive use on the overnight journey north. He and Lady Montmorency were to share one of the compartments, myself and Lizzie the other. The servants, Pearce and Millie, would have the small sitting-up compartment at one end of the carriage, adjacent to Lizzie and myself, ready for any call we might make on their services.

We stood on the platform as a porter stowed our luggage away in the van. It was a warm summer's evening, but I was glad of my fur travelling cape, and pulled it snugly around me. Lizzie caught my eye.

'The trains are so cold at night, aren't they?' she observed. 'I am glad Sir Horace was able to use his influence to provide us with a sleeping-saloon. Foot-warmers are of little enough use in the depth of the night, with draughts from the carriage window and one's fellow-travellers in and out at every station.'

'I do like my bed,' I confessed. 'Give me a fine bed of goose down every time, with a quilted comforter.' And better still a young gentleman to keep me snug, I silently added.

We inspected our berths, and found them admirably equipped – as fine as many a ship's wardroom. I had never slept on a train before. Indeed, such carriages had not long been introduced on our railways, and I was pleasantly surprised by the luxuriance of the appointments, the marble washstand and the gleaming brasswork, the comfortable beds which had already been made up by the railway servants.

'We'll be away in a minute,' Sir Horace proclaimed, consulting his pocket-watch. 'I'd advise you to take your berths now, to avoid any delay. We stop at York, and Pearce has telegraphed ahead so that hot coffee and a hamper will be awaiting us. The crush of the refreshment room is abhorrent to me, especially at five in the morning.'

With that he turned on his heel and ushered Lady Montmorency into their own compartment. Lizzie made herself comfortable, while I stretched out on my own divan. We heard the guard's whistle, and with a jerk we were off.

Soon we were running smoothly through the northern environs of the metropolis. Lulled by the clickety-clack, clickety-clack of the wheels, I felt my eyelids beginning to droop. I had only had two or three hours' sleep the previous night – not that I regretted it, for it had been an evening of the wildest debauchery – and I felt ready to surrender myself to the arms of Morpheus already. I got out my portmanteau from beneath the divan and was quickly changed into my nightclothes.

I peeped out from between the sheets to watch as Lizzie undressed herself. Such a firm young body! Such long, colt-like legs! I caught a glimpse of the pinkest nipple as she removed her chemise and closed my eyes in wonder. What a wonderful creation the human form is, I marvelled, as my fingers traced their way around my belly and towards my dark, thickly-bushed pussey. My thoughts went back to the previous evening, and Lord Somerville's unashamed delight on being confronted with my own nakedness. How his manhood had risen in salute! How he had pumped me so urgently, and spent his seed in a delirium of ecstasy! And I, too, had bounded against his great throbbing member, and matched him thrust for thrust, and shouted my abandon to the world –

and to the great amusement, no doubt, of those who were engaged in similar sporting frolics in the adjoining chambers. With my finger rubbing softly against the wetness of my pussey, I drifted effortlessly into warm and welcoming sleep.

We must have been somewhere near Grantham, I should imagine, when I was awakened by the most curious noises from the compartment next door. Sleepily I opened my eyes, to be confronted by the sight of Lizzie, attired only in her retiring robe, with her ear pressed closely to the wall of the carriage. Night lights bathed our compartment in a soft, golden glow.

'Hush!' she giggled, as I made to ask her what was afoot.

I made imploring gestures to her, but this served only to increase her merriment more.

'Listen for yourself, my dear Jenny,' she said at length, in answer to my silent plea. 'I'm sure I never heard anything quite like it in my life.'

I scrambled out of bed, and soon my ear was pressed up against the thin panelling that separated our luxurious compartment from the rather more spartan accommodation provided for our servants next door.

I listened for a minute or more, for it was difficult to ascertain exactly what the commotion in the adjoining compartment might be, what with the wheels flying so swiftly over the rail joints as we sped northwards. It was a strange mixture of bangs and muffled thumps, as though someone were shifting a large sack of flour around in that confined space. But why would anyone wish to do so strange a thing, at two in the morning and while travelling at fifty miles an hour upon the Great Northern Railway?

I listened again, harder this time, and soon I could pick out words and even whole sentences above the clicking of the rail joints. In a trice I knew what was afoot.

'The saucy devils!' I exclaimed, and caught Lizzie's eye.

'Perhaps we should see what is afoot,' she replied, and I sensed a hot flush had stolen over her pretty features.

She stood up, and indicated a small hatchway, not more than a foot square, that was set high up in the partition, no doubt the better to effect communication between the two compartments. It could easily be reached by standing on the end of one of the divans.

Holding our breath, barely daring to make a sound lest it should reveal our presence, we gently eased open the little sliding door and peered through into the servants' quarters, our faces pressed so closely together that I could smell Lizzie's sweet perfume.

On the horsehair bench opposite us sat Pearce, his nightshirt drawn up around his waist. Kneeling down in front of him was Millie, and in her hand she clasped the stoutest member that, I believe, I ever had seen in my life – nor, for that matter, have had the great good fortune to see since. Her tongue flickered playfully around her lips for a second or two before she began a lascivious game of licking the purple tip of Pearce's swollen manhood.

'Take it all in!' I heard him exhale, oblivious to our presence. 'I'll soon have a wollopin' stiff-stander to give ye a damn' good rooting with!'

Millie took him at his word. Lizzie's eyes almost seemed to pop as she watched the young minx verily gobbling up his ivory staff. This way and that she played with it in her mouth, now sucking deep, now licking only the very tip with the softest tongue of velvet. Pearce ruffled her hair as she did so, imploring her to do his bidding – a task for which she seemed to need no second urging.

'Now!' he called at length, 'let's see if I can give you another fine bellyful of spunk!'

I glanced at Lizzie, and we winked knowingly. Pearce might not have quite Mr Tennyson's ease with expressing the language of romance, but with as fine a tool as that which Millie was now caressing, who cared for the niceties of expression? Evidently this was not the first time, that evening, that he had treated Millie's pussey to a good spunking. So that was what all the commotion was earlier!

He pushed Millie face downwards on to the seat of their carriage and pulled up her nightclothes, tantalisingly exposing her pink and well-rounded bottom to our astonished gaze. My hand, I noticed, had involuntarily strayed to the dark fur that fringed my already yearning pussey.

'Now then, you young minx!' he breathed. 'What would you like now?'

'Oh, your cock, dear Pearce. Give me your fine young cock. Push it right up me and spunk me as hard as you can, just like you done before.'

In a second he was behind her, kneeling on the floor, and as she spread her legs for him I could see her hand steering that ivory rod to that magic warm place between her thighs. His handsome young face was quite red with effort as he struggled to push that huge prick into a fanny that, I fancy, had seen very little of Mr Priapus until Pearce came along.

'Oh, I'm so *full*,' called out Millie, throwing all caution to the winds as she bucked and swayed in time with his urgent thrusts. 'Fuck me hard, you randy devil. Fuck me with that great big prick of yours . . .'

I glanced down, and was hardly surprised to notice that Lizzie was unashamedly frigging herself as she watched this fine young couple engaged in the lists of love. She caught my gaze, and blushed hotly. On a wild impulse I threw myself to my knees and nuzzled against her soft dark bush. My tongue probed her secret recesses, tasting the salty liquor of her sex; it had been some months now since I had last licked a woman's cunt, but my tongue had lost none of its art.

'Oh, Jenny!' she moaned. 'It's wicked! We shouldn't! We shouldn't! But I love it so!'

My senses reeled as I nibbled on her darling little clitty, and a lustful abandon coursed through my veins. I thought excitedly of the fine young couple we had watched fucking, and of the beautiful young thing I was gamahuching like a woman possessed.

'What are they doing now?' I beseeched Lizzie, before kissing those crimson lips again with all the urgency of a young buck embracing his sweetheart.

'She is on her back now, with her legs around his waist. See! How she bounds up to meet his prick. Oh, lick me, Jenny! Surely heaven can not hold such pleasure! Now he is lifting her up in his arms, pulling her towards him. Oh! What a fine cock he has! I would so love to lick every last inch of it, to taste his creamy spunk! Now he is standing up, clasping her to him, pressed against the carriage door. I am sure every signalman along the line can see them! I can see his thick cock as it thrusts in and out. Oh Jenny! She is coming! He is coming! I am coming! Oh, lick me, lick me, or I die!'

She gave a great shudder, and my tongue was

bathed in sweet spendings even as I rubbed my face against her ecstatic cunny. She shivered, and shook, and shivered again, and we fell all in a heap on to the divan. Lizzie looked at me with winsome eyes, as if to say, how wicked we were! Perhaps it was the first time she had known the delights of woman gamahuching woman. But I cared only that the servants in the compartment next to us had heard nothing of our recherché eroticisms. It is an item of common knowledge, that servants are not to be trusted with confidences, and it would never do for rumour to circulate. So as discreetly as I could manage, I rose to my feet and quietly closed the shutter in the partition.

Lizzie, I now noted, had fallen into a gentle slumber. I pulled the comforter over her lissom young body and – though I yearned still for the thrill of illicit loving – returned to the bed I had woken from but a few precious minutes previously. Vowing that this would be by no means the last time that I would taste the sweet, loving juices of Lizzie's delightful cunny, I allowed myself to drift off into sleep.

Some hours later, we arrived at the great railway station at York. It was still quite dark, but Lizzie and I quickly dressed and made ourselves presentable. How Lizzie blushed when first I greeted her upon awakening! But I kissed her brow, and stroked her thick blonde hair, and lovingly assured her of my utmost discretion.

There came a knock on the door, and Millie entered our small compartment bearing a welcome tray of food. Her face scarcely betrayed evidence of the passionate encounter we had witnessed in the early hours of that summer morning. But her pussey, I found myself wondering, must surely be sore after those two frantic bouts with Cupid's battering ram.

'Here's your breakfasts, Miss Lizzie and Miss Jenny,' she announced, bold as brass. 'There's coffee, and cold bacon sandwiches, and cake. Lord and Lady Montmorency are having theirs already next door. His Lordship says the day seems set fair, and we'll be in Edinburgh before noon.'

Was there a twinkle in her eye? I rather thought so, as I took the cup she proffered me.

Between us Lizzie and I quickly polished off our morning repast. Pleading that she was not yet quite awake, my companion lay down on her divan. I stepped out on to the platform. Our train would not depart for another ten minutes, and I was anxious to stretch my legs and take in the bracing morning air.

I had almost reached the end of the platform when I thought I spied a familiar figure. His back was to me, for he was deep in animated discussion with the guard. Suddenly he turned, and I knew him at once.

'Why Jenny!' he called. 'How extremely pleasant to meet you!'

'And how pleasant it is to see you, Captain Wilks,' I replied. The last time I had met Captain Marcus Wilks of the 2nd Suffolk Battalion, I had thought my cunny would never recover from the mighty stretching his thick prick had given me.

'You are bound for Scotland too, I take it?'

'Yes, we are with Lord Montmorency's party. We have a sleeping carriage to ourselves further down the train.'

'How absolutely extraordinary! Old Montmorency's invited me to shoot with him as well, wouldn't you know? I shall stay for a week at his estate, but then I must be back with my regiment by the twenty-first. We sail for Egypt the following day.'

We strolled along the platform together in the grey light of dawn. It was delightful to meet such an old and intimate acquaintance, in such surprising circumstances. I told Marcus so, and he spun round and caught me by the arm.

'You know, dear girl, that I've always held a bit of a torch for you,' he murmured in my ear. 'That night we spent at White's Hotel will live on, in my memory, until my last day on earth. Why, if I wasn't engaged already to dear Effie Frobisher, I'd have asked you to marry me there and then!'

'You flatter me, Marcus! But I'm sure you're only teasing. Effie is such a dear sweet thing, and such a great friend of mine.'

'Aye, but she can't suck a fellow's cock like you can, my love. Nor yet will she swallow his spendings as gleefully as you did that evening. But then there are few whose pussies have quite such a powerful nip on them as hers! I'm sure my Effie has quite the tightest little honey-pot this side of the English Channel.'

His talk quite made me flush with excitement, especially since the events of the early morning had left me in a peculiarly lecherous frame of mind.

'You didn't complain when I rode a fine St George on you that night,' I suggested playfully. 'I'm sure you told me that mine was the most delightful pussey you had ever sported with.'

'Ah, men always say such things, when they are rolling and tumbling a fine young girl.'

'Nevertheless, I'll wager that for powers of nip my pussey has quite the beating of Effie's. The bigger the prick, the harder I can squeeze it. I'm sure I could prove it to you, if you had a mind.'

We had practically reached our compartment

again. Millie and Pearce were packing the breakfast things into a hamper, to return to the station hotel. Lord Montmorency stood on the platform, consulting his gold half-hunter.

'Why, a good morning to you, Jenny,' he called as I approached. 'And bless my soul, is that not young Wilks with you? How do ye do, sir? I had expected you would travel down later in the week to our estate.'

'Indeed I did too, sir,' exclaimed Marcus, shaking hands with his Lordship. 'But I was able to get a day or two's extra leave, and being as keen as yourself to get out with the ghillies I decided to travel at the earliest opportunity. I was just checking our time of departure with the guard when I chanced to encounter Miss Everleigh here.'

'Aye, well, we'll be away in a minute,' said Lord Montmorency. 'You must take your seat quickly, Sir, or you'll be left behind. The Scotch Express waits for no man!'

With that he stepped into his own compartment and slammed the door. At that moment the guard's whistle blew.

'My goodness!' cried Marcus. 'My carriage is right at the far end of the train! I will never be able to reach it in time!'

'You old slyboots,' I teased him. As no one was looking, I gave the front of his trousers a gentle squeeze. 'You'll have to travel with me. But there is a problem . . .'

'A problem?' His face, which had lit up in delightful anticipation, assumed a sudden frown.

'Oh yes. I'm travelling with his Lordship's daughter, Lizzie. But I'm sure a fine young military man like you has more than enough spunk in him for the two of us.'

And as the train moved off I quickly bundled him into our compartment and slammed the door.

I made hasty introductions of Captain Wilks to Lizzie, and Lizzie to Captain Wilks. Lizzie looked slightly taken aback at the sudden disruption of our travelling arrangements: was she thinking, perhaps it would preclude the possibility of another of our delightful Sapphic romps? But Captain Wilks' ample charm and handsome good looks soon won her over to his side.

For a while we made pleasant conversation as the flat fields of Yorkshire flew past the window. Captain Wilks produced a small volume from the pocket of his travelling cape, and was soon engrossed in its perusal. Lizzie and I talked of this and that, but soon I began to feel bored and restless.

'What's that book you're reading?' I enquired of our new companion.

'This? Oh, nothing. Actually, it's one of the classic studies on artillery, if you must know. You wouldn't want to look at it. It's deuced dull to read, but a chap in my position must keep abreast of military thinking.'

I knew all too well the kind of howitzer that was Captain Marcus Wilks' favourite subject for study. On an impulse, I reached across and snatched the book from his grasp.

'Here! Give me that!' he ejaculated. But I was too quick for him, and was soon leafing through the leather-bound pages.

'Artillery, eh?' I chuckled. 'I'm sure that bulge in your trousers is not caused by your attempts at calculating the trajectory of a cannon-shell. Here, Lizzie, listen to this.

*"Charley took off my bonnet and shawl, then my*

frock, stays and petticoats. I begged hard to be allowed to retain my smock, but all in vain as the Parson said it would interfere with the full view of my naked body; besides, he said: 'Eve was naked in the Garden of Eden, so there's Scripture for you' "

'Jenny, you are a minx,' exclaimed the handsome young officer when I had paused for breath. 'I told you you wouldn't want to read it. Now give it here.'

'Not so fast, Marcus,' I cried. 'There's more to come.

"*I was rolled over and over, their hands roving over my back, shoulders and bosom, belly and bottom in succession, one pointing out to the other some special attraction that he specially admired.*

"*My mouth and both hands were next occupied with three pricks at once, and I was obliged to change from one to the other, until each had his prick sucked.*'

'Splendid stuff, eh, Lizzie?' I laughed, my eyes greedily scanning the page of this remarkable book. 'But wait! Listen to how it goes on.

"*Next I was seated between two of them on the edge of the seat. Then they raised my legs higher than my head, and told me to jut my belly well forward. This had the effect of exposing my bottom-hole as well as my cunny. Then one gentleman would fuck me in this position and then the others would change places, until all three had fucked me. But I will say, they all withdrew their pricks before spending and spouted their sperm over my belly, as it was solemnly promised by them all that there should be no risk of getting me with child.*" That's sensible of her, isn't it, Lizzie? Where on earth did you get this rubbish, Marcus? It really is the most appalling piffle! It has all the excitement of a week at my Uncle Woebegone's house in

Devon-shire, eating cold porridge for breakfast and watching the cows munching grass. I suppose silly old men have to resort to this when their pricks will no longer stand! But for a young gentleman such as yourself, in rude good health, well! I really am stunned.'

'Miss Travis,' he said at length, addressing Lizzie. 'I really am most frightfully sorry about all this.'

But there was a hot flush on Lizzie's features. Her eyes gazed at him dreamily.

'You shouldn't read about that kind of thing,' I admonished him as sternly as I could. 'Where on earth did you get it from? Surely to goodness you didn't pay money for it?'

'As a matter of fact I paid that old bugger of Barnard's Inn Bookshop, Trevor de Souza, a silver sovereign for it last week. All the fellows like to read a sporting story, don't you know? And this one was almost as good as *The Oyster* but there were no further copies of that excellent magazine left for sale.'

I stood up, took a step towards the window and tossed the offending volume – which in truth I had really rather enjoyed, Mr Somerville in particular having a fine collection of such esoterica which we would often look at together while engaged in the lists of love – down the embankment as we sped by.

'It really was very wicked of you, you know,' I wagged my finger at Marcus, who looked as stunned by my action as a drunkard who lets drop his last glass of ale. 'We young ladies might be deeply shocked by those libidinous ramblings. As for a rascal like you, Marcus, I'm not surprised at the deleterious effect it has had on you. Why look, Percy is quite straining to burst out from his breeches.'

Now it was the Captain's turn to blush.

'Yes,' I went on. 'I'm sure we don't want any of us to be hit in the eye, should one of your fly buttons come shooting off. For shame! I think you should give both of us a good fucking by way of penance.'

He looked up at me, and then at Lizzie, and I fancied I saw a fierce longing in his eyes. Suddenly he burst into hoots of laughter.

'Why, Jenny, you are a tease! I never knew so saucy a girl! Nor young Miss Travis here, whom I swear has set my blood afire since I first set eyes on her.'

He was beside me in a flash. Quick hands fumbled with my clothes. I felt myself being pushed backwards on to the divan, and his breath hot against my face. Pushing him away from me for a moment, I loosened my petticoats. He gazed in rapture at my abandoned posture – above my grey kid boots I was wearing powder-blue stockings, and pretty garters of grey lace – and at the deep hairy cleft that was now revealed to him between my thighs.

He fairly tore off his trousers and drawers. A splendidly stiff cock bounced into view.

'Quick, Marcus, get your beautiful prick into my pussey,' I cried. 'Let's see what stuff you soldiers are made of.'

He was upon me instantly. I guided that ruby-tipped engine between the pouting lips of my sex and threw my legs up around his buttocks. Oh God, he was so huge, so filling, so utterly delicious! I had never wanted a cock more in my life, and I told him so. I felt the muscles of his body working frenziedly as he pumped in and out of me, and I matched him thrust for thrust. The motion of the train as we hurtled over points and around the curves only added to our pleasure.

'Harder, you devil!' I shouted in my rapture, bouncing up to meet him as he responded to my lewd urgings.

'Let me lick your tits, Jenny,' he panted. 'Lick your tits even as I fuck you.'

I scarcely knew what I was doing as I hastily undid the front of my blouse. The splendid cameo brooch that Lord Montmorency had given me as a birthday present would, I fear, have been lost forever had I not somehow had the presence of mind to slide it under the pillow. I pulled aside my chemise and in a trice he had buried his face between my breasts.

'Suck my titties, then, you randy devil!' I called out for all the world to hear. 'See how my nipples stand proud. Ha! Do you remember the night when you sucked one and Teddie Pickforth the other, and I played with your cocks until you both spunked all over my belly?'

'My God, Jenny, you're a right 'un!' he cried, and he drove me wild with the tickling of his moustaches against my hot pink aureoles, all the time that great cock working in and out of me until I felt I must die of the torment.

'Fuck me now!' I cried, knowing he was nearing his end and I mine. 'Fuck my cunt and tits! Let me feel your spunk spurt!' And then the world dissolved into a million shimmering fragments as his hot juices shot into me and my own quivering pleasure took me on and on down that dark lewd tunnel of lust.

We fell apart, gasping for breath. As I made to refasten my blouse, I noticed how Lizzie looked on longingly. I nudged Captain Wilks.

'Don't worry, Lizzie,' I murmured. 'I'm sure there's spunk enough for you too, once Percy here has regained his vigour.' Percy's owner nodded his assent. I stopped down, and licked the tip of the captain's wilted manhood.

'Oh, yes,' breathed Lizzie. 'I feel so wonderfully rude. I never did see a couple sporting together before, though I have sometimes watched myself in the mirror.'

'Come over here, my dear girl, and sit beside us,' beckoned Marcus Wilks, whose breeches lay on the floor still around his ankles. 'Better still, why not remove your skirt and petticoats, like Jenny here.' Lizzie did as she was bade, and we two girls snuggled up against our beau.

'Just let me light my cigar, my dears, and I'll tell you a story,' said Marcus. He produced a fine Havana, and was soon exhaling a cloud of blue smoke which quite made Lizzie and I cough. His hand, I noticed, had slid down between Lizzie's thighs, and he was gently stroking her pussey even as he smoked.

'Now it's funny you should mention watching two people fucking,' he began. 'Until a few months ago, I must confess it was something I had never even seen myself.'

Lizzie and I exchanged glances. I knew of old what a fine story-teller Captain Wilks was.

'Well, it so happened that I was on leave for a few days, and had come up to town to see my fiancee, Effie Frobisher. As luck would have it, I received a message that Effie was indisposed – an infection of some kind, with a fever, which had confined her to bed. As there was some degree of danger that the illness might be contagious, I was advised not to visit Effie for a day or two, and instead I sent flowers and messages of sympathy. Well, this was obviously deeply disappointing to me – I had come up to

London in a high degree of anticipation of some rollickin' good fun with her, and here I was confined to barracks, so to speak. Never did a chap's balls ache so, if you'll pardon the language of a military man, Miss Travis.'

I found it singularly amusing that Marcus should apologise to my friend for a momentary indelicacy of speech, when I could see with my own eyes how she had parted her legs the better so that he could insert a finger or two into her well-bushed cleft. But still ... As he resumed his narrative, my own fingers played lightly with the hairs on his manly chest, and over his small brown nipples, which perked up in a sprightly way at my touch.

'At length I resolved to go myself to the Frobishers' house, and present my compliments in person. The servant who answered my ring at the door-bell reassured me that the fever had now abated, and that if I would care to wait a minute or two – my fiancée being at that moment in the company of the family doctor, who was in the process of making his daily visit to his patient – he was sure Miss Frobisher would be delighted to see me.'

'She's spoke of nothing else but your comin', ever sin' she fell ill,' he told me. 'When she were in the 'ight of 'er fever, she'd a'cry out agin and agin "Oh do come, Marcus, oh do please hurry up and come." I knew what she was talking about in her delirium, of course, but I'm damn' sure the servant didn't. Effie was always one for hot dreams.

'Anyway, the servant suggested I wait in Effie's own private sitting room upstairs. The fire was lit there, while Effie's mother and some of her charitable ladies had taken over the downstairs living room and I had no desire to discuss the plight of the indigent poor with half-a-dozen worthy ladies of Kensington. So I took the servant at his word, and was shown into Effie's chambers.

'I could hear the murmur of restrained conversation between Effie and the doctor through the half-opened door of her bedroom. I was so looking forward to seeing my dear girl again – I had been away with my regiment on manoeuvres, and it had been a full three weeks since we had last met. In the end I could restrain my impatience no longer, and peeked around the door. And what do you think I saw?'

He paused, and drew luxuriantly on his cigar.

'Go on, then, Marcus,' I exclaimed. 'Don't keep us waiting. Tell us what you saw.'

'Why don't you suck my prick while I tell you?' he said. 'It does give a chap quite a tingle just to think of it, don't you know.'

In a flash Lizzie had taken his fine young cock in her mouth, and was rolling her tongue around its tip. Captain Wilks stroked her glossy auburn hair while he fondled my breasts with his free hand. We flashed through a station, and I hoped that none of the porters or passengers on the platform – it being now seven in the morning, and broad daylight – could see our wanton display.

'Chap was only giving her a damn' good rogering, wasn't he! I took a squint round the door of milady's boudoir and all I could see was the fellow's arsehole bobbing up and down. Gave me quite a turn, I can tell you. Funny thing was, I felt a bit miffed at first, as any chap would, but then I didn't seem to mind so much. In fact, I rather took a shine to watching this other blighter shagging my future wife. Met him before, once or twice – fellow called Gilbert Harding,

122

pleasant sort of chap, very good doctor – but never thought there was anything between 'em. Effie had told me his wife was a bit po-faced and she'd wondered if he wasn't maybe going a trifle short in the old how's-your-father department, but I never dreamed my Effie would be the one who'd want to remedy the deficiency. The chap's about my age, quite good-looking in a studious sort of way, but he's barely half my height after all, and Effie says she goes for the taller gentleman.

'So there I was peering through the crack in the door with a prick like the barrel of a thirty-two pounder, and there's Effie and this Harding fellow thrashing away like some agricultural steam machine, and eventually he gets up off the bed and takes his leave. I had to think pretty sharpish at that point, I can tell you. Luckily the curtains were drawn to keep out the light – strong sunlight always gives Effie one of her headaches – and so I dipped behind them. I heard the doctor leave the room and go downstairs. I waited a minute or two and then I went into Effie's room as though I'd just come up the stairs myself.

'I think she was a bit startled to see me – well, who wouldn't feel slightly taken aback, with their future husband standing before them, and half a pint of another man's spunk in her cunt – but she looked so radiant there with her hair in disarray and her clothes *en deshabille* that I threw myself upon her, and in an instant was myself fucking in the good doctor's spunk. Never did I enjoy a shag more! I'd not even frigged myself for a week at least, and my ballocks were ready to burst. My spendings fairly flooded out on to Effie's thighs, and on to the sheets.

'Afterwards, Effie burst into tears, and told me of her shame. She told me I was a good man, and she was now unworthy of me, and being momentarily in an intimate situation with the doctor – whom, she now confessed, she had long held a candle to – she had fallen prey to a rash indiscretion. But I laughed, and told her I loved her still, and loved her even more for fucking other men, especially while I watched. And she said that she had always taken rather a letch to being watched while she was being fucked, and had often thought of watching me fucking another woman, or of me watching her being fucked, that we both grew quite heated once again, and ran two further courses of abandoned pleasure before the booming of the luncheon gong bade us make our way to the dining room.'

'Oh Captain Wilks!' moaned Lizzie when he had finished his story. 'I'm sure I never heard anything so lascivious in my life! Do me the favour of plunging into my pussy that capital stiff-stander of yours, which I have sucked so hard that my mouth is quite sore.'

In a trice he had pushed her on to the divan, face downwards, so that her plump bottom cheeks were exposed to his lecherous gaze. 'My God, woman, I'll give you a rogering you'll remember for a week or two,' he cried as he threw himself upon her from behind. Lizzie pulled up her knees beneath her, and wiggled her arse lasciviously, as she presented her warm bum for his delectation. Without further ado the Captain plunged his hot, throbbing shaft into her quivering quim, and soon was pounding away with renewed vigour as Lizzie bucked and swayed beneath him.

'Here, Jenny, let me poke my finger up your cunt as I fuck your friend here,' he cried. I was only too willing to oblige – nothing, it seems, delights a gentleman so much as to pleasure two ladies at once. Besides I knew that the frigging – at which the Captain, as I recalled, was a past master – would quickly induce the spending I so assiduously sought.

With the Captain's strong thick finger poking around inside my sopping pussey I felt abandoned to my libidinous wants. Fired by the sight of his great cock as it thrashed in and out of my friend's quim I took on the extraordinary letch to push my own fingers in alongside it. I quickly acquainted my chums with my desire, to which they willingly agreed, and soon Lizzie's tight little cunny was stretched almost to bursting point by the double insertion of cock and fingers.

'Here!' I cried to my lewd paramour, 'Why don't you slap her bum while I frig you both!' The Captain needed no second bidding – it was, he later admitted, a particular favourite of his to smack Effie Frobisher's delicious little botty while she straddled across him, she meanwhile taking that great tool of his in her mouth and sucking him until he spent his seed. He uncunted, and I took hold of that great manly tool at the same time as I once again pushed my fingers into Lizzie's cunt which, by the by, was now well and truly dripping with the juices of love. Lizzie wriggled around so she could lick my cunt as I frigged her, while all the time the Captain's slaps resounded on her splendid bottom. With a girl's tongue playing with my swollen clitty – for no one knows better how a woman likes her cunt to be licked than another woman – I very quickly spent all over Lizzie's chin.

'Captain Wilks,' panted Lizzie in a voice that was by now almost inaudible. 'Would you do me the very great favour of putting that great battering ram of yours up my bum? I do so long to feel it there.'

I swear the captain almost came there and then in my hand. Quickly he rubbed the spendings from Lizzie's pussey over her wrinkled little bum-hole and his prick, the better with which to lubricate his entry into her fundament. And then he mounted up behind her and gently eased himself into her – for it does not do to rush the entry into that most narrow and private of passages – while Lizzie gasped aloud in surprise. Quick as a flash I leapt to my feet and began rubbing my bushy mound of Venus against the Captain's rump even as he buggered my friend – if it had grown any more swollen I was sure I could have pushed my clitty up Captain Wilks's own bum as I played the *frotteuse* against his arse. I reached my hand around his hips and played with his swaying balls and then, as hard as I could, I took hold of his glistening cock and squeezed. I could feel that mighty member throb and convulse as he jetted what seemed like a pint or more of spunk into Lizzie's bottom, Lizzie meanwhile squealing with delight as her own pleasure came upon her and calling out all manner of rude words which I had never before heard used by any other than labouring men of the commonest kind, to such effect that for the third time in but a few minutes I myself spent against the Captain's hard, muscular backside as the three of us collapsed in a heap together on the floor of the carriage, totally *hors de combat*. Fortunately, no guard came in to demand to see our tickets!

We finally reached Lord Montmorency's estate at four that afternoon, a little over eighteen hours since leaving the house in Hanover Square. In the bustle of the stop at Darlington, Captain Wilks had un-obtrusively quitted our carriage and made his way back to his own, leaving Lizzie and I to continue our journey alone.

His Lordship's Speyside property was indeed a most pleasing prospect to behold. As we clipped along in the carriage that had been there to greet our train at Boat of Garten, I caught a distant glimpse of that fine granite pile, lit by the late afternoon sun until it glowed like honey. As we drew nearer, I could see that the estate was surrounded by fine woodlands, with extensive cultivated grounds in which Lord Montmorency's guests could stroll at their leisure. A broad avenue of beech led from the gatehouse to the front of the house itself, where a fountain played as though to welcome us personally. Surrounding the fountain were statues of nymphs and cupids, executed in the finest marble.

Our apartments, too, were equally luxuriously appointed, and betrayed a knowledge of all the latest decorative fashion. I was delighted to see that Lizzie and I were placed in adjoining bedchambers. Captain Wilks, alas, was in quite another wing of the house, but I was sure that this would be no bar to our sporting escapades in the amatory stakes. Of the identities of our fellow guests I had but little notion. The Captain spoke of one or two chums of his who had been invited to shoot on the estate, but the bulk of the party would not be arriving until the following day.

Having supervised the unpacking of my trunks and valises, I hastened to inspect Lizzie's room at her invitation. Like mine it was most tastefully furnished, the walls a pleasing shade of *eau de nil* after the Chinese style and with many excellent pieces. A delightful oriental chest caught my eye; a maid had been packing away Lizzie's clothes in it, and one of the drawers was carelessly left open. As I casually pushed the drawer closed I noticed, in among Lizzie's silks and satins, a most unusual thing. An elegant carving of smooth ivory with inlaid silver filigree work lay in the drawer, and I paused to admire it. It was, I realised with a rush of blood to the head, a splendid dildo, the work of an artist and the property of a connoisseur of eroticism.

Lizzie knew immediately what had caught my attention – she had been in the act of tucking it safely down away from prying eyes when I entered unexpectedly – and blushed hotly.

'A very good friend of mine gave it to me,' the words of her confession came tumbling out. 'He was unfortunately obliged to travel abroad for some months, but gave me this exquisite keepsake to remind me of him.'

I picked up the dildo to inspect it more closely; it was some nine or ten inches long, and very thick.

'And is it an accurate replica?' I asked, rubbing the tip of the dildo against my cheek. I playfully licked it for a moment before handing it to Lizzie.

'Oh yes it is,' she said. 'It is almost as nice as having Harry's prick in me although this model was moulded from the erect cock of your old friend Sir Lionel Trapes, the wealthy roué of St Johns Wood in London.'

'Then I should like to try this marvellous engine for myself!' I cried. 'It has been some hours now since Captain Wilks deluged my pussey with his copious spendings and I am quite ready to run another bout.'

Lizzie and I embraced passionately. As my tongue sought hers, I realized how quickly she had been won over to the delightful sports of Lesbos. I am sure this Harry was far from being the only man to treat her to a pusseyful of cock, but am utterly convinced that our early-morning love-making aboard the speeding Scottish express had been her first introduction to the ecstasy of woman pleasing woman.

As Lizzie locked the door to guard against any unwanted intrusion, I removed my dress, stays and petticoats and lay down on the bed, dressed only in my pretty lace shift, boots and stockings. Lizzie did the same, and quickly we were kissing passionately, rubbing the bristling bushes of our curly pubic mounds together. Lizzie pushed a probing finger into my soaking cunt and I reciprocated, seeking out her sweet little button of love as she in turn sought mine with such delicacy of touch that I spent almost immediately. Next, Lizzie straddled over me while I licked her shapely pink nipples and then we enjoyed a delightful game of sixty-nine, excitedly licking each other's pussies until I felt I would die of the exquisite pleasure this brought on.

'Now, Lizzie, let me feel the delight of that splendid dildo embedded in me,' I breathed. I spread my legs wide in a wicked thrill of anticipation. Gently at first, but with an increasing firmness, Lizzie eased that cool ivory staff into my hot and welcoming cunt. I gasped with pleasure; Captain Wilks had a fine cock between his legs but it was no match for Lizzie's dildo in terms of size. I made a mental note to make the acquaintance of Lizzie's friend, who had so kindly made a gift of this wonderful instrument of ecstasy to her: I am sure that she would not begrudge me an hour or two spitted on his cock, especially if it were as satisfyingly huge as the dildo which was now pushed in me almost up to the hilt. It so completely filled me, in fact, that I begged Lizzie not to pump it up and down so vigorously; I felt sure I would burst, or be stretched so far that my famed abilities to nip and squeeze a gentleman's cock would be utterly lost to me.

'Let me lick your pretty cunt then,' she said, 'even as I work the dildo in and out of you. Why, I can pretend that it is Captain Wilks's cock, and that I am licking both you and he while you fuck together.'

It was the first time I had heard Lizzie use such words, and her idea quite inflamed me.

'Oh yes,' I cried in a transport of delight, as she suited the deed to the word. 'It is as though Captain Wilks is fucking me, and you are snuggled between us. What a fine thing that would be to do. You can lick my juicy cunt and then his stiff cock by turns. And then while we continued fucking you could let us both lick your cunt at the same time, and your sweet spendings would trickle over our tongues.'

'Oh, yes, yes, my dear Jenny,' sighed Lizzie, as my orgasm swept over me like a tidal wave of longing. 'Let the three of us do just that, at our earliest opportunity.' And I lay back abandoned on the pillow she pulled the monstrous dildo out of my swollen, puffy cunt.

'And look, my darling,' she cried, holding up the miraculous engine of love. 'I will then take the captain's cock in my mouth like this, and suck it as hard as I can, and frig myself just as I am doing now while you watch me, and then when my own spending comes upon me his seed will spurt and I will swallow it down like the wicked, greedy girl I am.'

It was a remarkable sight to behold: this demure aristocrat's daughter, from one of the highest families in the land, spreadeagled on the bed naked but for boots, stockings and garters, sucking a huge dildo in an ecstasy of make-believe as she wantonly frigged herself until she, too, fell exhausted into my arms.

Dinner was served late that day, at six o'clock, and we thus had plenty of time to recover from our abandoned sports and refresh ourselves. Montmorency Castle, I quickly discovered, more than justified its reputation as an epicurean paradise. Our repast that evening resembled nothing so much as a banquet designed to flatter a potentate: poussin stuffed with quail's eggs, followed by fillet of lemon sole, a splendid sirloin of beef, a sorbet, a pâté of venison on a bed of mushrooms, a cream pudding, savoury and cheeses, all accompanied by the very finest of clarets and white burgundies from Lord Montmorency's extensive cellars.

'And very soon we will be eating the first of the new season's game birds,' Lady Montmorency confided after the gentlemen had left us. 'Of course it is always best that they be hung first for a week or two, although I always relish nibbling at a fresh young breast in season.'

Lizzie and I could scarcely help giggling and winking at each other at her Ladyship's *faux pas*, but none of the other ladies present – there were but five couples at present in residence at the Castle, in addition to Captain Wilks and a dyspeptic old gentleman who was Lady Montmorency's uncle – seemed to pay any heed. Apart from ourselves, all the other ladies were considerably older and their menfolk had held little attraction for my roving eye as I inspected them during the course of dinner. However, I was assured that a number of gay young couples would be arriving the following day ready for the commencement of shooting on the twelfth, and I was eager to see what potential they offered for sport on my terms.

We took our coffee in the hall, an impressive chamber hung with ancient banners and coats of arms. Despite the time of year, a fire crackled and spat in the high carved hearth, for the thick stone walls of the castle imparted a chill to the interior. It was not a castle such as I had perhaps been expecting, an ancient fortress bristling with towers and ramparts, but this I now realize was only my young and fertile imagination at work – inflamed, perhaps, by too much reading of Lord Byron's work, and in particular *The Prisoner of Chillon*, the poet being on account of his passionate nature an especial favourite of mine. Montmorency Castle was instead a large building of substantial but pleasing aspect, built three hundred years ago by Montmorency's ancestor, Edward, Laird of Clockerty, as his family's country seat. Despite the Scottish Baronial style of its architecture, it was in great part similar to the country houses of England where I had been lucky enough to stay on my earlier tour.

Our game of Bezique over – Lady Montmorency and I had won three rubbers to two by our opponents, the Dowager Lady Gusset of Charnos and Lizzie, her niece – we made ready to retire for the night. It had been a long day, and though I did not regret the excitement of the previous evening, it had left me tired and quite ready for my bed. As we rose to bid goodnight to each other Captain Wilks came over to me. I half wondered if he were about to propose some scheme of libidinous adventure for the night; I would, I must confess, have been hard-pressed to resist his advances but I was so deadly tired from the exertions of the last twenty-four hours that I was rather shamefacedly relieved that he evidently had nothing of the sort in mind.

'Here, Jenny,' he said, looking quite pleased with himself; he had been taking Lord Montmorency's brandy quite liberally. 'Here's a little something for you to study tonight.'

'I fear any prospect of studying is quite out of the question this evening, Marcus. I am quite exhausted by the events of the day, and my eyelids are beginning to droop already. I am sure my body will have surrendered itself to sleep even before I lay a lock of my hair on the pillow.'

'As you please, my dear. But do take this anyway.' He handed me a small packet.

'I hope this isn't another of your filthy little books, Marcus,' I whispered to him.

'Nothing of the sort, dear Jenny. This is something much more artistic, the work of a very close acquaintance of mine, who will be arriving tomorrow. I know you have a keen interest in the arts and before you meet my friend Tom – he will be with us not long after breakfast, having travelled overnight from Edinburgh – I'm sure you'd like to have seen something of his work. He is much in vogue among the *cognoscenti* and aesthetes of London.'

Feeling slightly confused by the Captain's enthusiasm, I took the proffered packet and bade everyone good-night. When I reached my bedroom I put it on my bedside table and quite forgot about it. Soon I was tucked in among the sheets, but sleep did not come as readily as I had hoped. I tossed and turned, lay this way and that, but still the arms of Morpheus eluded me. The rhythm of the train seemed to run through my head still – I hoped I would not suffer from the head-ache – and I thought again of the remarkable scenes Lizzie and I had witnessed in the servants' compartment of our sleeping salon. Some lines of Lord Byron came to me, I know not why, and thinking how oddly they reminded me of my dear Lizzie I quietly recited them to myself, hoping this would lull me to sleep:

'Tis true your budding Miss is very charming
But shy and awkward at first coming out
So much alarm'd, that she is quite alarming,
All giggle, blush; half pertness and half pout.

But still I lay awake, and the candle by my bedside flickered fitfully. Feeling the need to piddle, I rose from my bed and used the commode. I was just climbing back into bed when my weary eyes lit upon the package Captain Wilks had given me. Expecting to find some small pencil sketches perhaps, or some lines of verse, I opened the envelope with no great curiosity. All this changed, however, when my eyes lit on the contents.

Here was a photograph of a lady sitting quite naked in her bath-tub, glancing playfully at the camera. Now a gentleman and a lady, not the same one, sitting on the edge of a bed. She is holding his erect tool; he is fondling her bosom. Her nipples, I noticed, were surprisingly large. Next, a shirtless gentleman appeared, tied to what were evidently the balustrades of a staircase. A girl, quite naked, has her arms around his shoulders; another kneels at his feet. In the next portrait the two girls are licking his nipples as he looks away, disinterestedly. In the third of this group one girl kneels down and has presumably taken his cock into her mouth; the other straddles over her shoulders, her cunt rubbing against the nape of her neck, and is passionately kissing the gentleman, whose interest has now evidently been violently reanimated. Now I found a series of *poses plastiques* of ladies in a boxing ring; then a lady, fully dressed for a change, admiring her private parts in a mirror. I gazed for a long while at two delightful girls, twins evidently, as they took it in turns to lick one another's bottoms; each to her own taste, I supposed. But my greatest surprise was reserved for a series of photographs which showed a gentleman and a lady larking playfully on a sofa: cocks, cunts, titties and bottom-holes were openly on view, as were the participants' faces. One was my good friend Effie Frobisher, and the other was unmistakably that of her fiancée and my lover of the previous night, Captain Marcus Wilks of the 2nd Suffolk Battalion.

Aflame with reckless energy, my heart pounding and my pussey soaking wet, I frigged and frigged myself looking at the photographs over and over again, my fingers sliding in and out of my juicy cunt. When I had spent three times, I fell into a deep and dreamless sleep and the flame of the candle guttered and went out.

The twelfth of August dawned bright and sunny. I woke to the sound of guns and looking out of my bedroom window – it was a little after eight o'clock – I saw a small group of men with their dogs near the wood that bordered the road. It must have been Lord Montmorency and his friends, for his Lordship had been scarcely able to conceal his impatience to be out shooting since we had assembled at the railway station two nights before.

When the maid had brought hot water I dressed quickly and knocked on Lizzie's door. She too was up and fully clothed.

'What a splendid morning this is, to be sure!' she cried, her face radiant. 'Did you sleep well?'

'Oh yes,' I replied. The crisp night air of Scotland had helped, of course, but after spending three times in a row I am sure even the direst insomniac would sleep like a top.

'So did I. And with good reason too – but I will save the description for later. Let's just say I had the most effective sleeping-draught I have ever taken administered to me. But come, Jenny, we are late enough for breakfast as it is. I have a hunger like a jackal this morning, and unless we stir ourselves, I am sure that Captain Wilks will have wolfed the lot. Never did I know a man with so prodigious an appetite.'

Nor so splendid a collection of erotic material, I thought to myself. I recalled that his photographer friend – who had so ably assisted me in my quest for repose last night – was due to arrive at any time, and I was anxious to make his acquaintance.

We breakfasted on cold beef from the night before, and kedgeree, and devilled kidneys. Only the dyspeptic gentleman we had met at dinner the night before was at the table – the other men were already out shooting, and their womenfolk were not yet risen from their beds.

'D'ye shoot yourself?' the older man asked at length through a mouthful of porridge.

'I don't, as a matter of fact,' I said. 'To be perfectly truthful, I think it rather an unpleasant business, to kill all those dear creatures in the name of sport. But I am sure it gives the gentlemen a good deal of pleasure.'

He appeared to disregard my remarks. 'My wife was a damn' fine shot,' he went on. His dentures apparently were loose, and rattled slightly in a clickety-clackety way as he spoke.

'But she passed on five years ago. Why, there was nothing she liked better than to bag a brace of pheasant before breakfast. She was a splendid fisher-woman too, and many's the fine salmon she's pulled out of Montmorency's waters.'

He went back to his porridge, which he attacked with unusual ferocity and then helped himself to a mountain of hot food from the tureens on the side-board. Lizzie and I exchanged pleasantries and made small talk between ourselves. Our companion quickly polished off his plate with a slice of bread and produced his cigar-case.

'Smoke, do ye?' he asked, offering a selection of cigars. Lizzie and I looked at each other in some confusion as he puffed out smoke.

'My wife always had a cigar after breakfast. Said it helped her bowels. Never noticed it meself, but she would say she could never move her bowels until she'd had her cigar. "Hubert," she'd say, "the best way to start the day is by emptying the bowels, and the best way to empty the bowels is by smoking a cigar first." It worked as well, at least for her.'

He rose to his feet, and carefully folded his napkin and placed it on his chair. As he hummed a military air his teeth clattered in harmony.

'I'll be away, then,' he said from the door. 'Nice day for a spot of shooting. Pity you two gels don't go in for it, though. If my wife were alive she could give you a lesson or two. Strange thing was, thinking about what we were discussing earlier, she always believed she could shoot better with a full bladder.'

As soon as he was out of earshot Lizzie and I collapsed into a fit of giggles. We learned later that the dyspeptic gentleman with the animated teeth was General Yardley, a senior officer in the Royal Army Medical Corps. As a young surgeon he had been a hero in the Crimean War of twenty years ago.

Later, once we had recovered our composure and finished our breakfasts, we took a stroll around the grounds of Montmorency Castle. At the rear of the house was a delightful parterre of green shrubs, with a promenade beyond which looked out over the parkland of his Lordship's estate. Lizzie and I found a seat in the sunshine and gazed for some time at the distant rolling hills and the shaggy brown cattle which grazed on the lush estate grass.

'Now then Lizzie,' I said at length. 'What was this marvellous sleeping-draught you were going to tell me about? I rather suspect that it was not liquid at all, but rather quite smooth and fleshy, and seven or eight inches long.'

Lizzie tittered, and blushed quite crimson; for a girl with such a lewd and wanton spirit, it was surprising how she often reminded me of Lord Byron's pert and pouting Miss in the poem I had recalled in bed the previous evening.

'Go on,' I said. 'There is no one to hear us apart from that herd of cattle over there.'

'Well, I had no sooner got into bed and blown out the candle than I fell into a doze. I do not know how long I was asleep, but I suddenly woke up with the suspicion that there was someone in my room. I was sure I could hear breathing, and then a muffled curse as the intruder stubbed his toe against a piece of furniture. I heard a sound as of clothing falling to the floor. I was much too terrified to cry out – in fact I pulled the bedclothes up over my head and hid beneath the blankets. The next thing I knew was not, as I feard, a pair of hands taking me by the neck, but rather that someone was climbing into bed with me.

'"Now then, my beauty," my unknown bedfellow murmured. "What did you make of my friend Tom's handiwork?"

'Of course I had absolutely no idea what he was talking about. But being half asleep, and wondering if it was not perhaps all a dream, I said nothing.

'"How'd you like to see some more of them, eh? I have a couple of fine albums I could show you when we return to London. Effie and I often look through them while we are in bed together."

'I realized with a start that the intruder must be none other than Captain Wilks. Now I knew it was a dream, and a delightful one at that. Nothing that had passed between us during the evening had prepared me for this unexpected visit, especially as I now realized that he was completely naked in bed with me.

'He put his arms around me and cupped my bubbies in his hands. At the touch of his fingers my nipples sprang up and I pressed my bottom against his stiff prick. He kissed my neck and shoulders and then quite roughly forced me on to my back. As I spread my legs for him he clambered on top of me and pushed that great prick of his right up me. Marcus is not nearly as big as my Harry, I believe, but then Harry's tool is so huge that my jaw fairly aches after I have sucked it for any length of time.

Though we have tried all manner of lubricants and patented preparations, it is quite impossible for me to take any more than the tip of it in my bottom-hole, and even then it hurts fearfully. But I took Captain Wilks's prick in my bottom with no difficulty at all, and I rather fancied having it there again.

'But I digress. Marcus pounded in and out of me quite violently, but the strange thing was that he several times called out your name, Jenny. I assumed this was some particular desire of his, and I took no offence. When Harry is fucking me he often likes to pretend that I am someone else, a lady he has seen at the music-hall, perhaps, or someone we have met – quite innocently, of course – during the course of the evening. Since it increases his pleasure so, I will gladly maintain the deception. Soon I felt my own pleasure coming on. Remembering how much he had enjoyed sucking your titties while he fucked you on the train, I whispered in his ear "Jenny would like you to lick her stalky red nipples for her, you wicked man. Let us see how much tit you can take into your mouth." He went quite frantic at this point, Jenny, and no sooner had he started sucking me than he shot his spunk into me as well and I spent copiously in return. "Oh, Jenny," he moaned as he rolled off me. "You do know what drives a fellow wild, don't you."

'I was quite flattered by his praise. Of course, I have known a prick or two in my time, but I have hardly enjoyed quite the amatory escapades that you have, Jenny. If he thought my performance was every bit as good as yours, then I was determined to repay him for the kindness of his compliments.

'When we had regained our breath I pulled the

bedclothes off us and then commenced to lick and suck his prick for him. How sweet the mixture of spunk and cunt-juices tasted! He tousled my hair as I did so, and said it was such a pretty auburn shade, and I knew he was off on his pretend game again, because my hair is quite blonde. Soon he had a capital stiff-stander.

'"Now then, Marcus," I exclaimed, still determined to maintain the pretence that caused him so much excitement. "I've seen you with your prick in Lizzie's little botty, and now I've taken a fancy to having it in mine."

'Soundlessly we slipped off the bed together. I knelt down over the blanket box at the foot of the bed and guided Marcus's stiff prick into my nether garden of delight. Before yesterday I had not been taken in this way more than twice in my life and now I had been buggered twice in twenty-four hours! Marcus was a little longer in shooting his spunk into me this time, but he played with my titties in a most inventive way as he fucked my bottom and also teased my clitty with his other hand, with such a finesse of touch that I had spent three times before he finally paid me the pearly tribute of his manhood, shooting a copious jet of creamy sperm inside my sopping cunney.

'Marcus was all for going to sleep after that, but I revived him by splashing him with cold water from the jug on the dressing table. I made him wash his cock and then I sucked him again to a stand. Inflamed by our amatory exploits, I was determined to experiment a little now. As I cupped his balls in one hand I pushed the tip of my index finger into his bottom hole.

"What's that?" he cried. "Hold fast, there! That's

141

deuced painful! You women have such long and pointed fingernails!"

His cry only excited me all the more. I pushed my finger in up to the second knuckle joint, and sucked his prick all the harder. Marcus writhed and thrashed around, whether in pain or ecstasy I could not tell.

"Hold fast there!" he beseeched me. "Ho! Stop or I die! I must surely lose my mind if this continues!"

'He almost pulled my hair out by the roots as he spent in my mouth – so much spunk he has in him, Jenny – and I triumphantly gargled on the white wine of love before swallowing it greedily down. It was impossible that he should spend the night with me in case the maids should discover us in the morning, so I slapped him playfully on the rump, pushed him out of the bed and bade him be on his way back to his own room. I heard him close the door softly behind him and that was the last I knew until I awoke this morning.'

'You are a wicked one, Lizzie,' I said after I had listened to her remarkable story. It was obvious to me that Captain Wilks was not playing a game, and that all along he thought he was in my room, but I hardly wanted to spoil her enjoyment of the night's frolics. She was such a dear and delightful companion, and any woman who can, during the course of one bout of love-making, be spunked in bum, cunt and mouth deserved my fullest admiration.

'It was a most remarkable evening, as I can certainly testify,' responded Lizzie. 'But the curious thing is, that rather than quench my appetite for such jiggery-pokery, it has made me even more lascivious. If our holiday continues in this vein, I shall be more than delighted. I now feel that if I am not fucked three or four times a day – and I care not whether it's a prick or a lady's tongue or Harry's dildo that's in me – I am unfulfilled, and out of sorts.'

We strolled along the promenade and out into the parkland. Away in the distance we caught the sound of guns. A flight of grouse came winging over from the direction of a small copse, and we decided to make our way thither, being careful, of course, that we should not walk directly into the line of fire.

Lord Montmorency's estate was, as I have suggested, one of the noblest in Scotland. Indeed, he had often played host to the highest in the land, especially during the shooting season, for he always made sure that game-birds were in plentiful supply for himself and his fellow enthusiasts. At the appropriate time of year there was also deer-hunting and salmon-fishing, though his Lordship always insisted that only that which was to be eaten should be hunted: he eschewed wasteful carnage, and there was a story that he had once openly remonstrated with the Duke of S*****a, whom he had caught blazing away at a bevy of plovers out of season.

We walked arm-in-arm along a broad avenue of elm trees. The day was set fair, and I was looking forward both to an invigorating stroll in the balmy Scots air and to meeting our new guests when they arrived. A train with a direct connection from Edinburgh was due at Boat of Garten shortly before noon, and I knew that a number of visitors to the estate would be travelling up on the overnight Scottish express, just as we had done. I wondered if any of them would enjoy such frolics as we had had – and indeed the two servants in the adjoining compartment!

The thought had barely left my head when we heard a rustle in an adjacent shrubbery. Intrigued

143

that this might be perhaps one of the delightful small deer with which the estate was populated, Lizzie and I crept forward on tip-toe. I peered around an azalea and there, to my surprise, was the very couple whose amorous exploits I had just been recalling.

Pearce and Millie – instead of being busy about their duties as good servants should – had taken advantage of the excitement engendered by the opening of the shooting season, there being already some twenty or thirty brace of grouse and woodcock brought back to the castle, and had slipped away into the parkland. I was left in no doubt that Pearce was, to use one of Captain Wilks's typically rumbustuous phrases, 'giving her one.' His trousers were round his ankles, while his buttocks thrust and squirmed there on the grass before us, while Millie – her legs wrapped tightly about his waist – bucked and heaved in answer to his urgent promptings.

Lizzie and I winked at each other, and under the cover of the shrubbery we crept closer, the better to view the spectacle. So engrossed in themselves were the servants, however, that had a herd of elephants come charging through the shrubbery I doubt whether they would have been disturbed.

Spying a pile of sturdy twigs that had been left behind after the gardener's diligent pruning, a lark of our own suggested itself to me, and I whispered my scheme to Lizzie. Taking a switch each, we waited until Pearce and Millie were almost at the height of their passion before rushing forth from our place of concealment.

'How disgraceful!' I cried, swishing at Pearce's splendidly muscular backside. 'How dare you enact such depravities before your betters! Have you no shame, man?'

Lizzie, too entered into the spirit of things, and lashed at Millie's bottom. The switches were still very green, however and would hardly have caused much discomfort to the two.

Pearce protested, and rapidly uncunted. When he tried to stand up, however, I swished away at him further. I felt awfully mischievous, having interrupted him almost at the moment of ecstasy, but I knew that this would hardly be the last opportunity he would engineer to get his prick into the ever-willing Millie.

For an actress whose thespian experience had been limited to a very small part in a very bad production of one of Congreve's comedies at Montmorency Castle the previous year – amateur theatricals were then the height of fashion among the smart set – Lizzie was giving a commendable display of remonstrating with her maid for her bad behaviour. 'Really, Millie, I am quite ashamed of you. Take that! I have a good mind to report what I have seen to my father, and then where would you be, eh? This really is too bad. It is not at all the sort of thing one expects from servants, and certainly not when there are guests of the family in residence. Take that, and that, and that!'

Pearce and Millie looked very sheepish, and we felt genuinely sorry for them. Lizzie tossed down her switch, and told the offenders to stand in front of her. She then addressed them firmly with a wagging finger.

'Now look here, you two. Miss Everleigh and I have a very good idea of what was going on between you on the journey from Kings Cross the other night. I am sure that that was not the first time you have so indulged your carnal whims, either. Now we

145

find you acting like beasts again, and in broad daylight. Were my mother or father to have discovered you *in flagrante delecto* [Pearce looked blankly at this] I am sure you would have been instantly dismissed from their service. But as it is, with the house being full for the shooting season and as I have always been very fond of Millie, I am prepared to turn a blind eye to these disgraceful goings-on, on the strict understanding that there will be no repetition. Do you understand me?'

Looking very guilty, Pearce and Millie mumbled assent. With the shock and embarrassment, Pearce's great manly tool had, I noticed, shrunk down until it was no bigger than a small boy's tiddler.

'Now be off with you, and let us have no more of this. Miss Everleigh and I wish to continue our stroll in peace. Get yourselves back to the house and find yourselves something useful to do. And remember, don't let me catch you together like this again.'

While the unfortunate couple made their shamefaced – but now fully dressed – way back to the house, Lizzie and I collapsed into peals of laughter.

'Did you see Millie's face when she realized she was discovered?' gasped Lizzie. 'I thought she was going to die of shame, so beetroot-red did her face go!'

'Pearce's prick seemed to be trying to hide away inside him,' I added, 'so quickly did it shrivel up.'

Arm in arm we strolled towards the woodland.

'I would certainly hate it if I were to be interrupted at such a moment,' said Lizzie. 'But then, it is one of the risks one takes in frolicking in the open air.'

'Is that something you enjoy, then, Lizzie?'

'Oh, yes. Give me a barn or a hayfield any day! During the summer I used to while away the hours in a very merry way down on my uncle's farm in Devon-shire.'

'And what sort of capers did you get up to?'

'Oh, just the sort of things that young people everywhere get up to, if they are sixteen or seventeen and enjoy a spot of fun.'

'And what might that be?'

'Well, one hot July day . . .'

Just then there came a loud bang from close at hand, followed by another, and another. We had wandered much nearer to the shooting party than we had intended, and so we crouched down carefully in the hollow bole of an old oak tree lest we should get in the way of the sporting gentlemen. Hot in pursuit of game, they would not, I would have imagined, have been especially pleased to find two young ladies traipsing gaily about within firing range, and I said as much to Lizzie.

'You know that I am always game, nevertheless,' I quipped wittily. 'But I have no wish to be served up at luncheon, with my legs tied beneath me and an onion thrust into my private parts – although I remember Teddie Pickforth and I diverting ourselves in a not dissimilar fashion after a particularly lively wedding-breakfast at Brighton. The unusual feature about this anecdote was that Teddie himself was the bridegroom . . . But you were about to tell me a story of your own, dear Lizzie . . .'

'Indeed I was, Jenny, before we were so abruptly interrupted. Let us stay within the safe confines of this shelter until the gentlemen have passed by with their horrid guns. Now let me recall the occasion in question . . . Ah, yes. It was last summer, in fact, for we always used to spend the months of June and July at my Uncle Percy's farm in Devon-shire. Over

147

the years I had struck up a great friendship with some of the local lads. Grand boys they were, and we were all great chums, but it was all quite innocent.'

'You surprise me, Lizzie. Are you quite certain of your facts?'

'Well, I'm sure there was a little bit of "You show me yours and I'll show you mine," and that sort of thing, but nothing more. But as we grew older we naturally became more curious about each other. One evening we were sitting outside an old barn some way from the farmhouse. Pat – he was one of the boys – had brought along a flagon of cider, which they made on the farm, and he and the other boys, Robin and Thomas, were swigging at it like billy-o. I too had become partial to a drop as well, though cider is far more intoxicating than wine, I am sure.

'Anyway, we were larricking about and laughing when all of a sudden Pat kissed me and put his hand on my boson. I was not a virgin, but I was pleasantly surprised, for in those cloistered days I was not fucked more than once or twice a month, if that. Gently he played with my nipples through my white summer frock. Daringly I spread my legs apart as he did so, for I did not wear undergarments in the hot summer weather, and had taken the curious letch of wanting to let the others see my pussey as Pat and I embraced. Soon my frock was unbuttoned and my unstayed bosom revealed. I could see by the bulges in their trousers – for these were boys of good families thereabouts, not, as you might imagine, uncouth country boys in smocks – that my wanton display was having the desired effect.

'Pat licked and sucked my titties and then stood up and removed his trousers. His prick seemed

148

ready to burst. I suggested we would all be more comfortable in the hayloft, so we climbed up the ladder. The other boys took their trousers off too and soon we were naked together. Pat laid me down on a bale of hay and told the boys to take over for a while while he finished undressing. They came and laid down on either side of me and soon I had a prick in each hand and a pair of hands on each of my tits.

'When Pat was undressed he stood in front of me and pulled my frock over my head. I was lying there with my cunt soaking by now, dying for a spot of cock. The three boys studied my exposed pussey intently. "Lawks! Just look at that!" cried Robin, whom I am sure had not been with a woman before. "Why don't you lick it for me, then?" I said, flickering my eyelashes invitingly.

'"Oh, I wouldn't want to do that now, would I? It's dirty!"

'"No, it isn't! Lots of gentlemen and ladies – the highest in the land, indeed – love to lick and suck each others' privates. Look, watch me suck Thomas's prick now. Did you see that? Right, you lick my cunt and then I'll give your prick a good sucking too."

'Inflamed by my bold words, Robin slid to his knees and started to gamahuche my pussey with his tongue. It was all too much for me – I was heated both by the novelty of the occasion and the copious draughts of cider which we had drunk – and I spent for the first time, soaking Robin's face and chin with my sweet juices, which he greedily lapped up like a cat with a saucer of cream.

'Pat meanwhile had lain down on the straw beside me, his prick close to my face. I rubbed the shaft up and down for a moment or two and then sucked it greedily. I stretched my limbs out and soon there

149

were two boys licking my pussey while I sucked the prick of the third. I was desperate to have a prick in my cunt but the boys seemed to be enjoying themselves so much that I let them have their way. Besides, Pat then announced that no one was to fuck me until I begged them for it.

"Oh yes," I squealed as our tongues and private juices mingled, making me spend over and over again. "Oh how I would love to be fucked," I cried between mouthfuls of cock. I begged and begged, until my tormentors finally assented.

'Robin was the first. He lay down on top of me and his fine young stiff prick slid into my waiting, dripping cunt. I came again almost instantly, so glorious did it feel to have a prick in me at last. Robin was so excited by now that he did not last long, jetting his hot torrents of spunk into me which triggered me to spend again. Thomas almost pulled him off me and soon I was speared by his great weapon too. In no time at all a second load of spunk shot into me.

'Pat was standing by my feet as Thomas got off me, looking hard at my pussey. I could feel their spendings and my juices trickling out of my overflowing fanny and down my bum-furrow.

'"Looks nice, doesn't it, Pat," I murmured. "Feel how wet and sticky my pussey is now."

'He put his fingers into my pussey and drew them out again, all dripping and glistening with spunk.

'"Why don't you fuck that lot back up me," I cried.

'"Damn' right I will," cried Pat, and threw himself on top of me. He put his spunky fingers in my mouth and I licked them clean for him, while the others urged him on with lewd cries of encouragement. He had a fine big tool, did our Pat, and he evidently knew a thing or two about fucking, for he lasted much longer than the others, and diddled me this way and that, but soon my cunt was again awash with spunk.

' "How did you enjoy that?" he panted, when he had slipped out of me.

' "That did me very well," I replied. "You may fuck me as often and as hard as you please, all three of you." And so they did for the rest of my holiday in Devon-shire. They came in my mouth, over my tits and in my cunt so many times during the course of those few delightful weeks that there was more cream splashed over me than in all the cream-teas that were ever served in the county betimes.'

'What a delightful tale that is, Lizzie,' I exclaimed when she had done. 'I am all aflame to meet your friends from Devon-shire myself. What a shame that we are so very far away. But hark! Do I hear someone coming?'

Indeed I could. Voices were borne towards us on the wind, and there came the distinctively pungent aroma of a cigar. Though the main shooting party had moved off back to the house – it was nearly time for luncheon – here were evidently a couple of stragglers making their slow progress across the park.

'A capital tale indeed, sir!' boomed a voice that was unknown to me. 'It reminds me of the anecdote concerning a certain young gentleman who was out driving one day in his gig, in the company of a lady friend with whom he had not long been acquainted. All of a sudden, the horse broke wind violently. Not wishing to appear uncouth, he apologised handsomely, and said how sorry he was for this most unfortunate occurrence. The young lady rested her hand lightly on his for a moment, and looked softly into his eyes. "Pray do not concern yourself with such a trifling matter," she said to the mortified young man. "Had you not spoken of it I would have assumed it was the horse which was the cause."''

Roars of ribald male laughter accompanied this *bon mot*, and I recognised the voice of Captain Wilks. Emerging from our cosy nook in the bole of the old oak tree, Lizzie and I surprised that young gentleman and his companion as they strolled leisurely over the greensward.

'Why hello Jenny, and Lizzie too!' he exclaimed, evidently not suspecting that we had overheard the joke. 'Here is my good friend Tom Feather, of whom I spoke yesterday. Tom, Lizzie, Tom, Jenny. Jenny, Tom, Lizzie, Tom. Or should it have been the other way around? Dammit! Anyway, Tom was just telling me how fond he is of horses, weren't you Tom?'

'Eh? What? Oh yes, indeed, so I was,' said the gentleman in question, who was a handsome young man of perhaps two or three and twenty, with sleek dark hair and a splendid set of moustachios. Quite a thrill went through me as I studied his physiognomy through modestly lowered lashes.

'And do you ride, Miss Everleigh?' he asked.

'Oh yes, Marcus and I have it in common that we both enjoy riding as often as possible.'

Marcus, whom I happen to know sits in the saddle with all the grace and dignity of a sack of potatoes, looked at me with suitable astonishment.

'And the three of us have already enjoyed the pleasure of several rides together,' I went on.

'Really?' exclaimed Tom, drawing so fiercely on his cigar that the end glowed quite red. 'Then perhaps I might join you at some time? I'm sure we would make a fine foursome.'

Had Marcus been telling him something of our little escapades? Judging by the roguish wink which Mr Feather gave me as he made his suggestion, I rather suspected so.

'Tom's a photographer, Lizzie,' said Marcus. 'Jenny has seen some of his work already, and admires it greatly.'

'How very interesting,' said Lizzie. 'I have always wanted to try it for myself, but there seems to be such a fuss with all those plates, and chemicals, and dark-rooms that I have always felt quite inadequate to the task. Perhaps you could show me some of your secrets.'

'Delighted to, I'm sure. I have everything with me – indeed, I had to unload so many trunks and cases of equipment at the railway station that we had to leave it behind in the custody of the station-master, or there would not be room for us all in the carriage. Lord Montmorency's man had to make a second journey to fetch it all.'

'Old Montmorency wants Tom to photograph the party of guests,' interjected Marcus. 'There's no one local who has the skill, so he brought Tom up from London at my suggestion. Now, tell it not in Gath, but I've a pretty shrewd idea that a certain royal personage will be joining our party later in the week, to enjoy a day's shooting on the estate and then to be the guest of honour at the ball on Saturday. His Lordship, I rather fancy, was rather taken by the idea of having a real, one hundred per cent royal on the premises, and wanted a photograph of the occasion to show his cronies back in St James's.'

'It's nothing of the sort, Marcus!' protested Lizzie

laughingly. 'Father has been a great friend of the Prince for many years now, and he often comes over from Balmoral. He says the Montmorency estate has the better shooting!'

'You didn't tell me any of this,' I whispered to Lizzie at luncheon that day. 'Surely you'd have told me of so momentous an event?'

'Of course I would, my dear Jenny. But father only told me this morning. The Queen has been indisposed, and the Prince has been obliged to remain close at hand. It was feared that his visit might have to be postponed, but I am glad to say that our monarch is now quite well again and a message was sent from Balmoral to say that the Prince's visit would go ahead as planned.'

The Prince of *******, eh? I was certainly climbing society's ladder. Had you told me only a few months ago that I would attend a ball in the presence of Royalty – possibly even to be honoured by an invitation to partner him in a waltz – you could have knocked me down with the proverbial feather.

Speaking of which, I was delighted to see that Lizzie and our Mr Tom Feather – he of the matchless photographic skills – seemed to have struck up a great friendship over the luncheon table. Among the other guests the conversation consisted of shooting, shooting and more shooting, but wrapped in their little *tête à tête* they seemed to be oblivious of all this.

'Tom and Lizzie seem to have hit it off very well,' I happened to mention to Marcus as we left the luncheon table.

'Yes indeed,' he said. 'He is a splendid fellow, I'll say that. And how did you like his photographs?'

'Very well indeed, thank you. I cannot wait to see

some more examples of his handiwork. I told Lizzie all about them, and she is quite agog to make an inspection of Tom's pictures.'

'And so you both shall, my dear. But now I think I must go out and shoot something, or old Montmorency will think me a frightful spoilsport. I will have a word with Tom while we are out on the moor and see if perhaps a little something cannot be arranged for later this evening, if you so desire.'

'I most certainly do,' I said, *sotto voce*.

'Then I must be off. The General says the best birds are to be found over towards the open country.'

I whiled away the hours in pleasant and fruitful diversions, and made the acquaintance of a number of guests who had newly arrived from Town. Though most of the menfolk were already out on the moor, I was delighted to make connaissance of Miss Miranda Welsh, who with her parents had reached Montmorency Castle that morning, and who seemed a very spirited young filly. Another lady of great charm and beauty was the flaxen-haired Miriam, Countess of Courtstrete, while the great newspaper owner Mr Aubrey Thirkettle and his striking partner – 'Do please call me Angelica,' she breathed almost as soon as we were introduced, though I was scarcely on equal footing with any of the guests – were most amusing and stimulating company. Great patrons of the arts, they seemed to be on intimate terms with many of the great painters of the day. It was quite late in the evening – shortly after supper, in fact – before Lizzie, Marcus, Tom and I were together again in the drawing room. The day's sport had gone well, and many a fine bumper was raised as a toast. So many, in fact, that I formed the distinct impression that the majority of the company were, despite their exalted social position, more than a little the better for drink.

I had just finished a rubber at cards with Miss Welsh, Mr Feather and the General when Lizzie came up and whispered in my ear.

'I've just had a word with Pearce,' she breathed as quietly as she could, 'and arranged that a few bottles of champagne be discreetly taken up to my room. After this morning's episode, I think the young devil owes us a favour – and I'm sure that we can rely on his tactful silence. If you could suggest to Marcus and Tom here that they might care to join us, I think we might round off the evening splendidly.'

All was quickly arranged. In due course the guests bade each other good-night, and Lizzie and I retired to her chamber. After a while, when all was quiet in the great house, we heard the tread of soft footsteps coming down the corridor. This time, I hoped, Marcus would manage to find the right room. Lizzie opened the door, and ushered in Tom and Marcus, who were holding their shoes in their hands lest they disturb the sleeping guests, although in point of fact, other than Lizzie and myself, only an old spinster aunt who was quite as deaf as a newell-post shared this particular part of the house with us.

'Now then,' called Marcus, uncorking a magnum. 'Who's for a glass or three of bubbly, then?'

We sat around most enjoyably for some time, sipping champagne and chatting of this and that of mutual friends and suchlike.

'Well then, Tom,' said Lizzie at length. 'Where are these famous pictures of yours?'

He produced a small envelope from his inside pocket, and passed it over. I craned my neck to see. I suppose there must have been very few sights enacted between men and women that Lizzie and I had not now seen with our own eyes, but Tom's photographs fairly beggared my descriptive faculties. The hugely endowed models, of both sexes, made us blush and giggle. Truth to tell, I am sure we were both greatly aroused by the pictures, which left little to the imagination, and when I suggested we might all like to make ourselves more at ease – to illustrate the point, I stood up and stripped down to my chemise and stockings – the other three followed suit, and soon we were practically naked together.

I smiled at Marcus, who was sitting beside me on the sofa, and asked if Effie liked the pictures too.

'She loves to pose for them,' he assented. 'But best of all she likes to read a racy book: *The Romance of Lust* for one, or *The Lustful Turk.*'

He put his arm across the back of the couch, and stroked the nape of my neck, something which never fails to arouse me to the highest pitch of longing. Tom and Lizzie, I noticed, were in an equally intimate pose. It was dark, save for the bright glow of the fire – though it was August, the nights were cold in the north of Scotland, and every bedroom in the great house had the fire lit at seven o'clock – and the warm golden light reflected in our champagne glasses.

I watched as Tom moved to kiss Lizzie. It was no delicate caress, such as a shy young man might give his first love, but a lingering tonguing that went on and on. I could see their mouths open and close, their lips pressed close, their tongues flickering and probing, while the pair of them in their passion pressed their bodies hard into each other. I saw Lizzie cling on tight, her bared thighs moving sensuously, her hands moving agonisingly slowly over his thighs and towards his privates. I opened my own legs, and Marcus stroked my soaking pussey with his long and expert fingers.

'You smell divine, my sweet,' he whispered in my ear. 'I am sure you wear the same perfume as Effie does. She buys it from Jermyn Street, I believe.'

'Does she now?' I murmured, intent on other things. I kissed Marcus hard and firm and thrust my tongue into his mouth. I felt his hands cup my breast and heard him moan his praises of my womanly bosom as I slipped out of my chemise.

When I turned my head away for a moment, I saw that Tom and Lizzie were lying on the tiger-skin rug before the fire. Lizzie had Tom's prick clasped in her hand and the pair were kissing each other hungrily. I watched as they pulled off each other's remaining garments and then they were naked together before my gaze. Lizzie's firm young bubbies bounced into view and Tom squeezed them together in his hands, kissing and sucking them. In a trice – for I knew how it excited Lizzie to have her nipples sucked – she had rolled over backwards, legs apart to show her mound of blonde bushy hair, and pulled Tom over on top of her.

I felt Marcus drawing my hand downwards towards his groin. His prick was iron-hard, its length and girth seemingly bigger than I remembered from previous occasions. I felt my cunny pulse and throb, as if opening wide in lustful anticipation. When I looked across the room again I saw a sight that aroused me still further. Tom was now astride Lizzie, and I heard her moans and passionate sighs as she lifted up her bottom in answer to his thrusts, her legs curled around his back. There was no doubt she was enjoying a right royal fucking, and enjoying every second of it. I turned back to Marcus with eyes half delirious with desire.

He kissed me all over my neck and face, then admired my breasts which he squeezed with both hands. He nuzzled and licked them, and playfully nipped the pink tips with his teeth. I sank down further on the couch, and Marcus paused to slip a cushion beneath my buttocks.

My legs were now wide apart, and Marcus stared hard at my cunt, bending down to kiss it as though it were still the ruby-red lips he had a moment ago been kissing so vehemently. His tongue flicked tormentingly along my parted slit.

'Oh Marcus,' I cried. 'Give me your ram-rod prick now!'

He was between my legs, the fiery red tip of his love-engine pushed hard against the dripping lips of my cunny.

'Beg me harder,' he exclaimed. 'I want to make you want it.'

'Oh yes, yes,' I cried. 'I want you to spunk me in my cunt. Fuck your big cock into my cunt, you randy devil.'

I gasped in relief as his fine hard cock slid into me. I felt as though I were transported somewhere else entirely, so completely did the waves of pleasure slide over me.

'Fuck it hard up me,' I heard myself call, as though I were someone else. 'Fill my cunt with creamy spunk. I'm aching to be fucked by a fine young cock like yours.'

As Marcus redoubled his efforts to satisfy me, I turned my head and saw Lizzie and Tom sitting up by the fire, their amorous interlude over for the moment, watching Marcus and I as we thrust and heaved. I decided to give them a display of wantonness and lewdness such as they might never have seen before in their lives, and I scratched, clawed, wriggled and squealed the most frightful obscenities to such effect that when I next turned my head Lizzie was hard at work sucking Tom's prick while he libidinously licked her willing cunt. The sight of my best friend so engaged with a man whom she had met barely twelve hours before, allied to the feel of Marcus's elephantine cock pounding away inside me had me rearing up my bum to match him thrust for thrust and I quickly spent in a delirium of desire and wantonness.

Even then our pleasure was not yet over, for we then changed partners and retired to our own rooms, where I am delighted to say that Mr Feather tickled my fancy to such effect that I spent and spent while we sucked, fondled and fucked the hours of darkness away. In the morning, as the rosy-fingered dawn stole through the curtains, my new lover stole away from me to regain his own chambers before suspicions be aroused, and I dozed in rapture for an hour or two of welcome bliss.

The next few days were spent in a most delightful manner. Several times Lizzie and I accompanied the gentlemen as they roamed the park and the adjacent moorland in search of game. From dawn till dusk, it seemed, the hills around echoed to the *crack-crack-crack* of gunfire. And many was the hip-flask that circulated among the company to keep out the cool morning air.

One morning, instead of going out with the guns, I was sitting alone in the library, writing letters to friends when I chanced to overhear a conversation between Mr and Mrs Thirkettle who were sitting on the terrace below, evidently thinking there was no one within earshot.

'I tell you,' said Mr Thirkettle, 'I'm all aflame to enjoy the delicious Jenny as soon as I decently can. And her friend Lizzie, come to that. I wonder if we can manouevre matters so I might be alone with one or other of them.'

'You are a wicked man, Thirkettle,' said his wife. 'If I didn't know already that you had no taste for such things, I'd thrash you within an inch of your life myself. It's been some days since I've had the pleasure of administering correction to an errant soul, and I feel a deep and terrible hunger is upon me. You're sure you wouldn't like a little caning yourself, just to take the edge off my appetite?'

'Quite sure, thank you, Angelica. Others may find flagellation as exciting and stimulating a prelude to sexual relations as any of the tricks a good French whore can play. For myself, I am afraid the only effect it has on me is to leave me with a damn' sore arse.'

'What a spoilsport you are, Thirkettle. I swear that were it not for that great fine prick of yours, and the remarkable length of your tongue, I would have divorced you long ago.'

At this Mr Thirkettle chuckled aloud.

'And had I known of your tastes,' he said, 'I might not have entered into so fruitful a marriage contract myself. I little suspected that I, for my part, had married a *flagellante extraordinaire*, a true mistress of the lash indeed. But what matter? You are no less sweet a person for all that, my dear Angelica, and I am desperately fond of you.'

'And I of you, you old beast.'

How extraordinary, I thought when they had

161

moved off. I never knew of such things, outside the confines of the public schools! With her splendid mane of dark hair and rich blue eyes – to say nothing of her remarkable knowledge of artistic matters – I would scarcely have thought Angelica Thirkettle was the strict mistress of the lash which her conversation had suggested. I had, I must confess, but little idea of what a mistress of the lash *should* look like, but I was quite sure that she would not look like her. But then, outward appearances can be so deceptive. Who would have thought that, with his fresh, ruddy complexion and honest yeoman's features, the gallant Somerville with whom I had spent the night before our departure for Scotland was not only one of the youngest members of the House of Lords but was also – far from being a simple rustic shagger who learned his craft from watching the animals in the farmyard – a lover of great finesse and inventiveness, who had brought me to spend three times before we had even fully undressed.

My thoughts were interrupted by the arrival of Mr Feather. I greeted him effusively, for he was splendidly jovial company as well as a lover of great accomplishment and, of course, a highly talented artist. I wondered, did the aesthetically-minded Thirkettles know of his work?

'What ho, Jenny!' he exclaimed, being so bold as to steal a kiss from me in the otherwise deserted library. 'And how are we today?'

'Very well indeed, thank you.'

'And Lizzie, is she well? Marcus says she's got a fit of the vapours, but he's not much of a judge of a lady's moods, I'm afraid.'

'Miss Montmorency was a trifle out of sorts, this morning, I must confess. But I think she's had so little sleep these past few nights that it's beginning to tell on her. She retired back to her bedchamber after breakfast this morning, and I'm sure a few extra hours' sleep will do her the power of good. You just wait and see, you naughty man. She'll have your prick in her mouth again before you can say "Angelica Thirkettle."'

'The fair Angelica, eh? She seems a sporting kind of filly, I'll be bound. I wouldn't mind a wager on her in the 3.15 at Chepstow, what? Ten guineas each way and Bob's your uncle, ha! The word is that she's something of a patron of the arts, and I wouldn't mind selling her a few of my photographs if I can. So many of these old fuddy-duddies wouldn't touch a daguerrotype with a bargepole, but I don't think she's one of those, somehow.'

'Oh yes, I'm sure both Mr and Mrs Thirkettle are very progressive in their views on art. But surely it's a portrait photograph you're thinking of, or a landscape. You can't be thinking of photographs such as those you showed us the other night.'

'I wouldn't be so sure, my dear Jenny. Only the other week, I had a gent came to my studio, a very high-up official in the Bank of England, he was, and what do you think he was after? Did he want a nice view of the Thames at evening-tide? Or a portrait of an old sea-dog at Greenwich, or an East-end flower girl? Not a bit of it! What he was after was snaps of black gentlemen, preferably ones generously endowed in a particular department. Naked men wearing boxing-gloves was something he especially sought. And if I had any pictures of black men fucking other black men in their bottoms, so much the better. "Be off with you, you dirty old bugger!" I said to him, cutting him off sharpish. "This is a

163

respectable establishment. Why, I have had commissions to photograph royalty, and I would certainly never stoop to such work as you suggest. Now begone with you, before I call the police. A respectable City gentleman like yourself, for shame! I shall take my bank-account elsewhere too.' Or I would have done, if I wasn't a hundred or two in the red . . .'

'But wouldn't that have helped solve your problems?' I enquired. 'Surely he would have paid handsomely for you to do as he suggested?'

'Of course it would – but I have a reputation to consider. What I did,' he went on with a conspiratorial wink, 'was to get a chum of mine to get hold of pictures such as he sought – and to charge the banker double. We split the proceeds, he got a hundred guineas, I got a hundred guineas, the banker got a nice portfolio of snaps which we'd bought for a fiver down near the docks – a pretty poor selection they were too, from Egypt I suspect – and everyone was happy.'

'And how do you find the models for your poses?' I asked, very interested in Tom Feather's novel art form.

'Oh, some are friends, and friends of friends, and some are gay ladies – but no streetwalkers, though they may be ladies of easy virtue they are all ladies of quality too. And artists' models too, of course. I was a portrait-painter before I became a photographer, and I know many delightful young models who are only too delighted to pose for me.'

'Is it very difficult?' I ventured.

'Not at all, though you have to learn the art of staying still while the exposure is made. That's but a few seconds though. Why do you ask?'

'Well, I was just wondering,' I said hesitantly, though I stammered for effect rather than out of any genuine nervousness. 'I was wondering if, ahem, you might like to take a photograph of me. In the nude, that is. I am sure I know of one or two young gentlemen who might like a print as a keepsake.'

Now it was Tom's turn to look slightly abashed. I am sure no lady worthy of the name had ever asked him to photograph her in the nude before purely for her own amusement.

'Why, erm, yes of course I would,' he exclaimed at length. 'Be delighted to, in fact. I've taken some twenty or more plates of Lord Montmorency and his party and there's no more work for me until the Prince of Whatsits arrives on Saturday. When were you thinking of . . .'

Just then our little business transaction was interrupted by the arrival of Captain Wilks, who came bursting into the library with a face radiant with the purest joy.

'At last,' he exclaimed. 'A letter from Effie! Here, Jenny, why don't you read it? I told you Effie was a bit of a minx, didn't I? Here's the proof of the pudding! I never knew of such goings-on, upon my word. I can hardly wait to write back to her and tell her of our own little exploits. But then writing's something that doesn't come terribly easy to me, so I suppose I'll have to wait until there's a dull evening to fill in – which I must say there hasn't been so far, has there Jenny?'

He gave my bum a roguish squeeze and handed me the letter. It was addressed from Southwold, in Suffolk, where the Frobisher family had a delightful summer residence which they used in season in preference to their somewhat stuffy apartments in Kensington:

165

*My darling Marcus* (Effie wrote in her own fair hand)

*I hope this letter finds you in such fine fettle as it leaves me! I swear my life of late has been filled with events of every imaginable kind, including some which would shock even you, my darling wicked man!*

Have I spoken to you of my new friend, Dolly Parker? Sweet, unaffected girl! We met when she was appearing at the Red Lamp Theatre in a quite outrageous French farce, to which I returned again and again, with some dear friends of mine.

Dolly played the part of an outrageously wealthy femme fatale, *though she swears in all innocence that she would never have accepted the role had she known its full implications. What a hoot! It is one of the naughtiest plays I have ever seen, and I'm sure, my delectable boy, that you'd have loved it too. Alas! It was forced to close when the theatre was invaded one evening by a band of burly police constables intent on spoiling everyone's fun. Meaty though some of these guardians of the law were, I really cannot abide spoilsports.*

*My friends and I escaped via the stage door, with Dolly in tow – which was how we met. Since then, well, Dolly and I have become bosom friends. And, my dear, I'm here to tell you that she provides enough front for the two of us! Despite her delicate, artistic sensibilities, – after all, they say that she's an actress of the very highest calibre, or at least Dolly herself does – she certainly believes in cutting a swathe with the gentlemen of our acquaintance.*

*I swear, sugar plum, that I've never seen a lower* décollétage, *blacker eyes nor redder, more glistening lips than those of my dear, sweet confidante. If I were a* girl with a nature other than that which God bestowed on me, I declare I'd be just a teensy bit jealous. In fact, sweetheart, I shall be keeping a studious eye on you both when you meet, which is practically assured since she's just dying to meet you on your return from Scotland, especially since I've told her all about you. Dolly being, as it were, between jobs at the moment as a result of the police's attentions, Father graciously consented to her accompanying us to our summer cottage. Judging by the looks he keeps giving her, I am sure even he is not impervious to her charms, the old fox.

Do you remember, my darling, the understanding we reached when last we met? I'd taken to my bed with a bout of something frightful and, in my helpless delirium, had been quite overcome by the charming manner of kind Dr Gilbert. (I swear he turned the colour of beetroot when we met again the other day, poor man!) Well, I feel compelled to tell you of a rather saucy incident which occurred just the other day, when Dolly and I pic-nicked at the seaside.

Dolly had brought along a hamper of the most tempting delicacies, which she had been sent by a gentleman admirer – a true connoisseur of art, according to Dolly, with the most impeccable taste; his name is Thirkettle, but I don't believe you or I know him. She and I were agreed that the sea breezes would sharpen up our appetites most wonderfully. Little did we know when we plotted our excursion exactly which appetites were to be whetted (or should I spell it wetted?!!). Have patience, angel, and I shall continue.

No sooner had Dolly and I found ourselves a nice, secluded spot among the dunes than Dolly produced a bottle of fine madeira from the hamper. In fact, Dolly seldom goes anywhere very far from a bottle or two of champagne or other white wine – she is a martyr to her nerves, you know. Soon we were overcome by a fit of the giggles and, like a pair of schoolgirls, we stripped off our boots and stockings and ran to the water's edge, where I'm sure our larks would have caused a stir had there been others at the seaside that day.

What a wicked pair we were, I am sure – both in our city clothes, though bare of leg; Dolly with her all-but-naked bosom heaving and panting and her splendidly made-up actress's eyes glistening and flashing with merriment and mirth; me with my dress quite wet and clinging to my thighs, my hair falling loose from its pins about my throat and shoulders!

We had been frolicking thus for about twenty minutes or so when, quite exhausted, we flopped down on to the warm sand, still quivering with peal upon peal of girlish laughter. As we gradually regained our composure, we became aware of the approach of a pair of gentlemen ornithologists, who had been busy observing through the powerful field-glasses they carried the activities of the various wading birds that made their home among the salt marshes and sand dunes. Our arrival had, unfortunately, so disturbed the birds that they had flown away.

Though understandably somewhat annoyed, they were soon soothed by our apologies – and Dolly's fluttering eyelashes in particular. They turned out on further acquaintance to be a most personable pair, both devilishly good-looking and not averse to a drop of madeira – in fact they both produced hip-flasks of cognac in which we were delighted to share. The least we could do in return – and to compensate for having so spoilt their morning's bird-watching by our thoughtless behaviour – was to offer to share with them our delicious luncheon. Plates of game pie, smoked salmon, cold meats, exotic pickles, trifle and chocolate cake were duly offered and consumed, together with enough wine to last a month of Sundays.

*Rarely, my love, have I enjoyed a meal so much! The effervescence of the champagne, which was of the very finest vintage, tickled my sensibilities to an alarming degree. The succulence of our repast, the warmth of the sun on our faces and bare legs and the novelty of the occasion – after all, it is not every day that one meets two such personable young gentlemen in so remote a situation – all combined to make Dolly and I fairly swoon with delight. So when our new friends took it upon themselves to make more freely with us than we might otherwise have allowed, we were quite powerless to refuse their amorous advances.*

*Dolly, for whom the heat had proved too strong, the wines too various and the company too exciting, has to this day refused to share with me the details of her experiences. She merely holds a trembling hand to her brow, closes her soot-black eyes and sighs deeply. I, on the other hand, felt more than able to entertain my new, handsome friend – their names, by the by, were Laurence and Roger, and the former was my particular favourite – and when we next meet, my dear Marcus, I shall furnish you with a full account, with practical demonstrations, of what went on in an hotel at Southwold that August afternoon.*

*My devoted love to you always*

*Your own sweet (but deliciously wicked) Effie*

'She's a corker, ain't she?' observed Marcus when I had done reading. 'I swear, I never knew a girl for such larks.'

'Her friend Dolly sounds a bit of a character,' I said. 'I must say I'm dying to meet her one day.'

'So am I,' added Marcus. 'In fact, I can barely

wait to enjoy a rollicking threesome. I'm sure Dolly is that way inclined – all these actresses are, I believe. But now, I must be out shooting. I must say, since we've been up here I've developed quite a taste for the sport. This morning, and for the next couple of days, we're shooting over towards old Abernethy's place. Lizzie's father is anxious to conserve the game closer to the house, so as to have plenty of birds around for when the Prince comes. He doesn't want to have to tramp miles over hill and dale in search of a solitary woodcock. How about you, Tom?'

'I think I'll give it a miss, old chap. I enjoyed being out with you for the last few days but there's a most delightful glen I spotted yesterday which would make a perfect landscape study. I'll think I'll wend my way thither if it's all the same with you.'

'All the more birds for us, then. Well, I must be off. Time waits for no man, what?'

'*Vis à vis* what we were saying earlier,' Tom ventured when Marcus had gone, leaving us alone once again in the library. 'I wonder if you might care to accompany me to the glen. Though it's but a short, pleasant stroll away, it's a perfectly secluded spot. It would make an ideal backdrop for a photograph such as you were speaking of, and the day is most delightfully warm. Unless you are otherwise engaged, of course.'

'Not at all, dear Tom. I would be delighted to accompany you. I will just return to my room for a moment and then I will join you. Shall I meet you by the fountain in twenty minutes or so?'

An hour later, with my hair freshly pinned and my face powdered, Tom and I set off for the distant glen. He carried with him his camera – a large affair of mahogany and brass, mounted on a sturdy tripod

– and a box in which he transported the glass plates on which he would make the exposures. Though his burden was quite a heavy one, he refused my entreaties to let me help him.

'No no, my dear,' he soothed. 'It would never do to photograph you when you were all puffing and blowing, would it now?'

The path to the glen was one I had never taken before. Indeed, so hidden was it from the house that I had not previously even noticed it before. Evidently it was as unknown to our fellow guests as it had been to myself, for though, as we looked back, we could see small groups of men and women strolling about elsewhere in the grounds of Montmorency Castle, we met no one on the path and the countryside ahead seemed entirely deserted.

After a surprisingly short while we came to the glen itself. A small, sparkling stream danced before us in the sunlight and the cry of birdsong filled the air.

'What a delightful spot this is,' I exclaimed, filled with rapture at nature's beauty.

'Indeed it is,' agreed Tom. 'I only stumbled across it by the purest happenchance. Old Montmorency told me he rarely comes down here to shoot, for there is poor cover for the birds, but that once in a while, if the weather were fine, they would pic-nick by the stream.'

We sat by the stream on a large rock, like lizards sunning themselves. Small clouds darted across the sky, so that the glen was now bathed in beautiful dappled sunlight, and then plunged into shadow, before the sun came through once more. Tom Feather was, as I have said, a most delightful and vivacious companion, with a ready wit and amusing line in anecdote, and I soon felt completely at my ease. He explained to me the workings of his camera, and of the various qualities of light, until I became quite sure that the photographer is in every way just as much a painter with light as is the artist with his easel and oils.

'Now then, my dear Jenny,' he ventured at length, screwing up his eyes to look at the sky. 'If I'm not mistaken the sun will be behind that big, anvil-shaped cloud for a few minutes now. Let me get my camera ready and by the time that's done the sun will be out and we'll be ready to take a picture of you just as you are, sitting on this rock.'

He quickly set up his tripod and told me how to assume the required posture. I leaned back against the rock, resting on one elbow with my legs tucked beneath me in an attitude of repose. Tom fitted a glass plate from his box into the camera and then, right on cue, the sun came out from behind the cloud.

Tom made some adjustments to the big brass-bound lens on the front of his camera and then disappeared under the black cloth.

'Just move your right hand a little, would you?' came his muffled voice. 'That's fine, yes. Now hold it like that, please, and keep exactly still.'

He removed the cap from the lens, and I heard him counting slowly. Then he put the cap back on the lens and emerged, a little red-faced, from under the cloth.

'Very good,' he said, as he busied himself with the plate. 'You can stretch a little if you like. I'll take another one from a different viewpoint now, so we can see more of the stream in the background.'

Again we went through the same procedure, and Tom pronounced himself delighted with the result.

'Now,' he said at length. 'Just slip out of your clothes, will you? The sun's at just the right angle now.'

Feeling a tingle of licentious delight, I quickly stepped out of my dress and removed my underthings. I had taken off my stays beforehand – it would have been terribly difficult to get them back on again – and soon I stood naked before Tom's admiring gaze.

'Marvellous!' he exclaimed when he saw his Venus disrobe before his eyes. 'You have a splendid body, Miss Everleigh, if I may be so bold as to say so.'

'You may indeed, Mr Feather. You have quite a handsome physique yourself.'

He laughed, and busied himself with his camera again. At Tom's instruction I assumed the same pose on the rock as before.

'Now,' he instructed, 'I want you, when I say so, to lean forward slightly and take a big, deep breath.'

'Why is that?' I asked, feeling slightly puzzled.

'It will emphasise the splendid swell of your bosom all the more.'

I was learning something every minute! Soon Tom was ready to make the exposure. At his command I assumed the position and Tom uncapped the lens as before.

'Splendid!' was his verdict. 'I am sure none of my professional models ever seemed able to pose so naturally.'

'Flattery will get you everywhere, you naughty man,' I told him, fluttering my eyelashes and wondering if they were as long and dark as Dolly Parker's.

'This time I want you to lean back on the rock a trifle more. That's right! Good! Now, will you part your legs a little?'

173

I did as I was told, exposing the soft pink cleft of my cunny to the camera's unblinking gaze. As Tom counted the seconds, I felt most indescribably wanton. I was delighted that the glen was so remote, for I would hardly want to perform this kind of thing in front of prying eyes.

'Now,' said Tom, 'let's see you splashing about in the stream like a water nymph in some ancient myth. Such a photograph would be very artistic, I am sure.'

With Tom's help I stepped out over the rough stones and into the stream. It felt surprisingly cold, for the day was particularly warm, and I was aware that my nipples had perked up by way of response. So too had Tom. They are, though I say it myself, a particularly splendid pair of nipples – Teddie Pitchforth once said he would rather nibble my nipple than a strawberry, though both were equally soft and sweet – and Tom was desirous of taking a head-and-shoulders portrait of me to show my rose-tipped bosom in all its majesty.

For the first pose, I stood with my hands raised up to the sky, as though I were some sun-worshipping ancient. Then I stooped down, as though admiring my reflection in the water. Finally, I posed on a large rock in the stream itself and at Tom's request opened my legs as wide as I could, leaning backwards and idly fingering my soft curls.

'That's marvellous,' he said as he put away his plates. 'You can come out of the stream now if you like.'

Instead, I danced up and down and splashed a great quantity of water at him.

'Be careful!' he cried. 'You'll ruin the photographs if you get impure water on them!'

'What could be purer than a mountain stream, you silly man? Come on in, and let us frolic together. I feel so stiff after posing for you like that that I need some exercise to stretch my legs. Looking at the front of your trousers, you must be feeling pretty stiff yourself.'

Tom laughed, and quickly divested himself of his clothing. Soon we were sporting naked together in the stream, splashing water and shouting and generally carrying on. I am sure the small fishes which I had seen darting in and out of the limpid rock pools must have taken to their hiding-places under the stones in fright.

One thing led to another. Before long, Tom and I were kissing passionately, standing quite naked in the middle of the stream. I felt his gallant cock stiffen against my stomach as I covered his neck and chest in kisses and playful bites. With the water reaching to our waists I wrapped my legs around his hips – he was quite strong enough to hold me thus, though the current swirled and eddied around us – and soon felt myself spitted on his splendid cock, which must I am sure have gained an extra inch or two in girth because of the cold. Our mouths met hungrily, again and again, and then Tom was sucking my titties as hard as he could. The sensation so electrified me that even as I spent in a wave of ecstasy I felt myself beginning to overbalance. The next thing I knew we had both toppled full length into the stream.

Gasping for breath, I looked around for Tom, but not a sight of him could I see. I glanced this way and that, but could catch no glimpse of him. I began to feel alarmed. What if he had been swept away, and drowned? Perhaps he had dashed his head on one of

175

the rocks with which the bed of the stream was strewn, and had been knocked unconscious. How quickly a rising tide of panic replaced my unbridled lust of but a moment before!

All of a sudden, strong hands seized me from behind, and I was borne roughly towards the bank and thrown face-down on the same rock where I had posed for photographs. Had I been taken by some strange water-beast, a serpent such as the famous monster of Loch Ness? I felt a scream beginning to well up in my throat.

'I'll teach you to splash water over my camera, and then give me a good ducking!' cried a familiar voice. 'Why, I was just on the verge of spending myself when you started throwing yourself about like a newly landed salmon!'

In a second I was speared from behind by Tom's rampant prick which slid into my cunt from behind. In front, his firm, manly hands squeezed and kneaded my breasts, and my nipples responded in their characteristic fashion. I felt his tongue brushing my neck, my shoulders, my ear lobes.

'Spunk me now, you water-devil!' I cried as his hips pounded harder and harder against me. I pushed out my backside to meet his powerful thrusts, and gave way to my wildest instincts. Surely this was how it had been for Adam and Eve, in the Garden of Eden, before the Temptation? I felt like a nymph in one of the paintings of antique scenes which hung in the hall of Montmorency Castle.

Later, we stretched out on the banks of the stream and dried our limbs in the sun. Then, warmly satisfied after another fine bout of fucking in the open air, we made our way back for lunch.

*

At dinner that evening I was delighted to make the further acquaintance of the Count of Courtstrete, with whose delightful flaxen-haired wife – Miriam by name – I had already enjoyed several games at cards. The Count was seated to my right, while on my left was Mr Thirkettle.

The conversation had turned to the subject of verse. I professed myself to be an admirer both of Lord Byron and of Mr Edward Lear, whose delightful Nonsense poems were all the rage in society.

'Yes, Lear is a capital fellow, I'll be bound,' said Mr Thirkettle, who was evidently an intimate of the gentleman concerned. 'He lives abroad now, for the sake of his health, but Angelica and I have often visited him when our travels have taken us to Italy.'

'He is also an artist of some note, I believe,' said the Count.

'Indeed yes, though not perhaps a painter of the first rank. My wife and I are nevertheless delighted to have one or two of his paintings in our collection. They are much admired by visitors.'

Captain Wilks was sitting opposite us, and listening intently to our conversation.

'Isn't Lear the chap who writes limericks, and such?' he asked.

'That's right,' I said. 'We were just talking about him.'

'What's the one about the young lady with the bonnet?'

'I'm sorry?'

'The young lady with the bonnet. Something about the birds sat upon it.'

'Oh, yes,' cried Mr Thirkettle. 'Let me think now:

There was a young lady whose bonnet
Came untied when the birds shat upon it
But she said 'I don't care
All the birds in the air
Are welcome to shit on my bonnet'

'That's the one!' exclaimed Marcus, who as usual
had been availing himself liberally of Lord Montmorency's seemingly boundless wine cellar. 'It
always reminds me of my fiancée, Miss Effie Frobisher. She's the kind of gal who don't give a damn
either . . .'

Mr Thirkettle looked anxious, as though I might
be offended by Marcus's language, but I assured
him with a wink that I was not in the least put out.

'She is a spirited girl, then, your Miss Frobisher?'
asked the Count.

'I should say so,' came the reply. 'Why, I had a
letter from her today in which she said . . . Ach!
Goodness me! I've cracked my knee a right one on
the table leg.'

I smiled inwardly, and drew back my foot. Marcus
was such a tactless fool sometimes, though I loved
him dearly. But he was not to be deterred from
making an ass of himself.

'I've got a limerick of my own, in fact,' he proclaimed. 'My Effie nearly burst her stays laughing at it
when I told her. Would you like to hear it?'

Such a course of events was inevitable. Marcus
was known in the Officer's Mess as a 'two-bottle
man' but I rather think some reassessment might
soon be required. Not without a certain reluctance,
we indicated our assent.

'Right, then! Now, how does it go? Let me see
now:

There was an old maid of Calcutta
Who purchased a steam-driven fucker
By the light of a candle
She cranked up the handle . . .'

The final line was lost in a flurry of embarrassed coughing from my neighbours and a scraping of chairs from elsewhere in the room. Mercifully, it was time for the ladies to withdraw, and I rather think that Marcus was given a 'stiff talking-to' over the port for his indiscretion in front of a lady. Such was the impression I got from the Count when we talked later over coffee on the terrace below the library.

It was a marvellous summer's evening, the birds flying high in the sky and the shadows stretching out like long dark fingers over the estate.

'I'm really not at all a prude, you know,' I said to him. 'Of course, I abhor vulgarity and uncouth behaviour. But I think our strict moral standards of today are rather false, wouldn't you say? From what I know of the eighteenth century they had a much more lenient attitude, one that did not so impair the true expression of feeling.'

'It depends on what kind of feeling you mean,' said the Count. 'The feelings of our great Romantic poets, for instance.'

'Yes, exactly. Lord Byron did not let convention and decorum inhibit the expression of his passion. If only more of us could feel the same way.'

'I am sure I agree with you, my dear. There must be rules, of course, or society will be plunged into chaos. But our present attitudes seem only to condone the narrow-minded views of a minority. Why, at times I feel quite a libertine myself by comparison.'

'And are you a libertine, Count?'

He looked at me in a quizzical manner. I had not noticed before, but he was handsome in a fair-skinned, almost Germanic way: he had a moustache on his upper lip, but otherwise was clean-shaven in the typically Prussian manner.

'And are you, Miss Everleigh?' he asked in reply, neatly evading my question.

'I'm not quite sure what you mean. Would you be more specific?'

'If I had said that, all through dinner, I had longed to drop my fork on the floor and, under the guise of recovering it from under the table, to kiss you most passionately about your dainty feet and ankles, would you say that was the behaviour of a libertine?'

'Yes, I think I would.'

'And if I said that I'd then like to kiss your legs, and draw up your dress, and part your long legs, and gamahuche your exquisite cunny until you spent in delirium, you would not deny that that, too, was the desire of a moral profligate?'

'Possibly, yes. But define yourself further.'

'And if I said that my wife and I have been longing to take you into our bed one night, so that the three of us may sport together, would you not look upon me with contempt?'

'Yes I would, Count, but in one respect only. You speak of three people, but I would insist on four. I would be delighted to extend the invitation to my friend Mr Feather over there, whom I know confessed to me just this very afternoon that he must surely soon go insane if your wife Miriam were not to suck his prick for him.'

'How extraordinary!' exclaimed the Count in a

voice so loud that I feared others would overhear our lewd conversation. 'Why, Miriam has several times told me she is longing not only to lick your cunt, but to enjoy Mr Feather's cock as well. What a coincidence! Shall we arrange it for this evening? We are in the west wing, but I am afraid our bed is quite a small one.'

'No, no. I am in the other wing, right next door to Miss Montmorency. Our rooms are very well furnished. Indeed, I am sure Lizzie Montmorency would be delighted to fall in with our plans, and we could form a happy fivesome together. Only the other night we enjoyed such a debauch – Lizzie, Tom Feather, Captain Wilks and myself . . .'

'I fear Captain Wilks will be unlikely to take part in any debauch tonight! I never saw a man drink so much wine, nor so much brandy! I believe I saw a servant helping him to his room shortly before we came out on to the terrace.'

It was arranged, then. The Count and Countess would come to our rooms on the pretext of inspecting the fine marble fireplace, or somesuch, and remain there. As soon as practicable after the company had retired, Tom would join us. I spoke with Lizzie – who was quite well recovered from her morning's indisposition, and was raring to be fucked again, not having had a prick up her all day – and she made arrangements with the obedient Pearce for a supply of champagne to be on hand.

Earlier that evening, Tom had shown me the results of his morning's work – he had spent the afternoon sequestered in the temporary darkroom which had been placed at his disposal. I have to say, I was most impressed by the results. Quite apart from the erotic content of the photographs, which

showed my nakedness quite unashamed, they were
so tastefully arranged and showed such sophistry in
composition, lighting and suchlike that I am sure not
even M. Rodin could have done such justice to the
human figure. This was, I am sure, art of a very high
nature, very far removed from the Egyptian post-
cards which, Marcus had assured me, pass from
hand to hand in even the best gentlemen's clubs. I
therefore besought Tom to bring with him his
camera and other accoutrements, thinking that he
might very well have a further opportunity to demonstrate his prowess behind the lens.

At a little after midnight that evening, the scene in
the east wing of Montmorency Castle would have
fairly beggared the powers of anyone attempting to
describe it with any more felicity than I, a mere
narrator of fact, would be capable of. Picture, if you
will, a chain of people sprawled in attitudes of wild
abandon among a litter of empty champagne bottles.
I was stretched out on the bed in Lizzie's room,
while Miriam, the Countess of Courtstrete, fulfilled
her wicked fancy of gamahuching my cunt while,
kneeling at the side of the bed, she was being fucked
from the rear by her husband. Lizzie was meanwhile
lying beneath him playing with his balls and, as she
did so, enjoying the sensation of Tom Feather's
sizeable prick lodged as far as it would go in her
pussey. I managed to wriggle around on the bed far
enough for Tom to suck my nipples into such a
glorious state of excitement that I almost wished he
would take a photograph of me there and then.
 Next, while Lizzie and Miriam gamahuched each
other on the rug by the fire, the Count lay down flat
on his back alongside them and I spitted myself on

his cock in a splendid St George. Tom – who had set up his camera while we refreshed ourselves with champagne after the first bout of love-making – took a photograph of us as we disported ourselves in this way that for sheer lewdness must, I am sure, have far transcended anything he had previously recorded on emulsion.

I then was taken by the idea of having Tom's prick in my bottom-hole even as I was fucked in my pussey by the Count. My friends were eager to see it done, and Miriam assured me that it was the most divine sensation, she having enjoyed the pleasure of taking two men at once in this way several times in the past. Once, she said, she had had two pricks in her cunt simultaneously, but her husband was at pains to point out that they were but young boys, and had only small pricks, and that only a woman with the very slackest cunt could hope to take in two pricks of any size.

'And besides,' observed Tom as he smeared pomatum over his cock and my bottom-hole, 'what man would want to fuck a woman whose cunt was so loose that it needed two pricks to fill it?'

To this we were all agreed. Once again I spitted myself on the Count's prick, and leaned forward so he could lick and suck my titties. Tom pushed up against me from behind and in a trice his cock was lodged in my bum. I urged him not to push too hard, but to ease it in gently, lest I should be over-stretched by the double insertion. Being a gentleman as well as an artist, he readily concurred with my wishes.

'What ho, Courtstrete!' he cried. 'I do believe I can feel your cock through the membrane that divides Jenny's bum-hole from her pussey! Well I never!'

'I hope you're not one of those arse-bandits, sir!' snapped the Count from between my bosoms. 'Kindly concentrate on fucking dear Miss Everleigh here, and leave my prick out of it.'

I was so amused by his words that I could barely stop myself from laughing out loud. Instead, I called out lewd words of encouragement, urging them to redouble their efforts. Soon two jets of spunk came spurting into me almost at the same time, which immediately brought on my own pleasure.

'Here Lizzie,' cried the Countess. 'Why don't you put your finger in my husband's bum while he's lying there? That's one of his favourite little letches, to be sure.'

'I've got a better idea,' called out Lizzie, and in a trice she had returned with the splendid ivory dildo to which I had been introduced some days ago.

She also brought over an elaborate harness of straps and buckles which she fitted around her hips. It was, I now realised, most artfully designed so that she could wear the dildo in it just like a man's prick.

'Now then, who'd like my great big cock in them first,' she demanded in a gruff masculine voice. 'You, Tom? Or you, Count?'

'Why don't you fuck me, instead?' chimed in Miriam. 'I've not had any but my husband's cock in me yet this evening and I crave a novelty.'

Lizzie was greatly taken by the idea of fucking a lady with her dildo-prick, especially one of such exalted rank as the Countess of Courtstrete. Her friend Harry had originally given the harness to her, she subsequently explained to me, so she could encule him from behind, this being a pleasure of which he was inordinately fond, although the idea of having a real prick in his bottom-hole was curiously abhorrent to him.

Miriam laid down on the bed and parted her legs.

'By jove, I must have a photograph of this,' exclaimed Tom, moving his camera to the bedside.

In less than no time Lizzie was between the Countess's thighs, working the dildo in and out of her as vigorously as if she were a man. It was a curiously exciting sight to see their breasts crushed together, and to peer between Lizzie's legs at their two cunts as they squirmed frantically against each other.

The Count pushed me roughly on to my back alongside Lizzie and his wife, and drove his prick into me so hard it made me gasp. He, Miriam and I kissed each other passionately, and then Lizzie leaned over and sought my tongue. Next, I took Lizzie between my thighs while the Count fucked his wife lying flat on the bed – she with her legs thrown over his shoulders in a gesture of the wildest abandon. No sooner had he discharged a month's reserve of spunk into her than Tom was on top of her instead, the sight of the four of us licking and fucking having driven him to such a peak of desire that his cock seemed swollen to twice its normal size and his camera was quite forgotten.

Our final couplings, before exhaustion and the numerous bottles of champagne we had consumed finally took their toll, consisted of myself fucking Miriam with the dildo while Tom put his prick up her bottom from behind, even as Lizzie sucked the Count's prick and swallowed his spunk when it came bubbling out. Lizzie then sucked Tom off while Miriam and I licked each other's cunts until we had spent several times, the Count meanwhile pushing the dildo into each of us in turn until we could spend no more. Tom, Miriam and the Count stole away – it was nearly four in the morning – and because her own bed was in a state of utter dishevellment, I took Lizzie into my own bed where we frigged and kissed each other for a few more wanton minutes until sleep finally overcame us.

Even though the Prince was expected to arrive towards noon, I found myself quite incapable of rising for breakfast the following morning. My head ached, my temples throbbed, and the normally mouse-like maid seemed positively to bellow her morning's greeting. It was as much as I could do to take a sip or two of hot tea, and to beg to be left undisturbed.

I was fortunate that it was common practice for young ladies to sleep together – all quite innocently – for the maid did not bat an eyelid when Lizzie's tousled head appeared from beneath the sheets. I dread to think what might have happened if she had gone into her young mistress's room and seen the chaos that ruled there. Lizzie murmured that she would get Pearce and Millie to sort out the mess, and then went back to sleep.

It was gone eleven when I finally managed to rise from my bed. After I had washed and dressed, I went downstairs in the hope of finding an odd crust or two with which to quieten my rumbling stomach. Alas, the breakfast things had all been swept away, and the house was as busy as a beehive with the preparations for the arrival of the Prince. By looking piteous, and holding my head, and complaining of feeling faint, I was at last able to prevail upon a kindly older servant to fetch me coffee and cake which I took on the terrace.

With some sort of food inside me, I began to feel a little better. I had just managed to focus my eyes on the headlines of that morning's *Times* when an apparition floated before me. It was the Count, but it might just as well have been Banquo's ghost for all the life that was in it.

'My God, Jenny, is that you? Oh my head! Let me have some of that coffee, if you please. My mouth feels like a Frenchman has been living in it.'

'That was some evening, was it not?' I ventured.

'Don't remind me. I have no idea what became of Mr Feather – we left him comatose on the great stairway, clutching the very last bottle of champagne. Do you realise, between us we drank an entire case of the stuff? When Miriam and I finally regained our room she insisted on making love yet again, so heated was she by what had gone before. I tell you, my prick is so sore this morning that it is agony even to attempt to piddle. Ach! This coffee's cold.'

Saying he would go and find a servant to make us a fresh pot, I was left to scan the pages of the newspaper once more. I had barely begun to read the court pages – which confirmed that, as I already knew, Lord and Lady Montmorency would this day have the honour of receiving His Royal Highness The Prince of W***s at Montmorency Castle – than a cheery voice hailed me.

'What ho, there, old chuck! What a fine morning it is to be sure! I feel glad to be alive, I do indeed.'

'Marcus? Can that be you?' I peered at him through bleary eyes. It was indeed our Captain of the 2nd Suffolks.

'And why shouldn't it be me? Are you expecting someone else, eh? Perhaps you and the Prince have arranged a little rendezvous?'

'Don't be an ass, Marcus. If you had a little more tact, you might see I'm in no mood for your nonsense

187

this morning. It's just that, looking at the state you were in last night, I little thought I would see you in such fine fettle this morning.'

'Last night? Last night? Ah, yes! You thought old Marcus had driven his coach and four well and truly over the edge, didn't you. He's gone and done it now, hasn't he, the drunken old sot?'

'Well, you did, didn't you? The Count saw a servant helping you to your room a little after nine-thirty. You should be in no condition at all this morning, let alone leaping about there full of the joys of living. Kindly do not shout so loudly, either. It fair makes my head ring.'

'Wouldn't you just like to know, my dear? Ignoring, for the moment, the question of why you, and the Count and Countess, and Lizzie and Tom Feather – whose face was, I swear, as grey as a roof-slate when I saw him an hour ago – are all so obviously delicate this morning, perhaps I should tell you why I feel so full of spirits.'

'Yes, I think you should. Why is that?'

'Because, despite what you or anyone else thinks, I certainly wasn't full of spirits last night. Other than a glass of two or wine with the meal, I hardly touched a drop. Now, you all *thought* I was as drunk as a lord – *apropos* of which, by the by, old Montmorency certainly knows which end of the bottle to drink out of, my goodness me he does – but in fact I was as sober as a judge.'

This was beyond me. Hadn't I seen Marcus, with my own eyes, making a chump of himself as only a man in drink can?

'Come off it, Marcus! If you were sober last night, I am Miss Jenny Lind.'

'Then sing for me one of my favourite airs, my

dear Jenny, because it's perfectly true. I only wanted to *pretend* to be drunk, so that I could then slip away unnoticed as early as I decently could, and so that no one would think to disturb me later. I am afraid I had a secret assignation last night.

'An assignation? With whom, pray?'

'With the divine Miss Miranda Welsh. Oh, how my heart soars when I speak her name! I am sure I am quite in love with her already.'

'With Miranda? But you have hardly spoken of her before. How long has all this been going on?'

'Since the day before yesterday. Do you remember, when you and Lizzie went for a carriage ride and Tom was taking his picture of the shooting party over the yew-hedge? At that very hour I was abed with Miss Miranda Welsh, and making arrangements for a further assignation of a similar nature. This was where I was last night.'

'Knowing that her aunt, who has the next room, is but a very light sleeper, it was plainly impossible that I should spend the night with Miranda. However, the old girl so enjoys a game or two at cards that she rarely comes to bed much before half-past eleven or so. Miranda bid me come to her room early, so that we could enjoy an hour or two together in perfect security. She would plead a head-ache, or some such womanly complaint, not so severe as to require the attendance of a doctor but sufficient to ensure she could take to her bed in the early part of the evening and be left undisturbed.

'Now, no-one expects a man, least of all a military man, to be laid low by something as trifling as a headache. Over-indulgence is, on the other hand, something of a way of life here at Montmorency Castle. I therefore made the pretence of being a little

189

the worse for wear and staggered off to bed, muttering that I had better sleep it off in my own room rather than further abuse his Lordship's generous hospitality.

'No sooner had the servant left me in my darkened chamber than I was off down the corridor to Miranda's room. "Who is it?" she cried faintly in answer to my tap on her door. "It is I," I hissed. "Come in then, you wicked man," she purred.

'In a flash I was undressed and in the bed with her. Goodness, what a sport she is! She was dressed in but a pretty white lace camisole, with blue ribbons, and a pair of blue stockings which, with their garters of white satin ribbon, perfectly complemented her cornflower-blue eyes and thick blonde hair. Her bum and thighs were quite bare. I tell you, Jenny, my prick shot up and I almost spent there and then. Instead, I threw myself upon her and fucked her long and hard, and as our tongues played with each other we murmured endearments both sweet and lewd as we reached our climax.

'Before I had got my breath back – for Miranda bucks and sways like a young colt – she had my prick in her mouth sucking off the drops of spunk that still clung to it. Then in turn I licked my way down her body, from her exquisite pink-tipped titties down across her firm flat belly to her pussey itself. And what a pussey it is! Lips of pure vermillion framed in as delightful a thatch of pure blonde curls as one could ever hope to see. A delicious fragrance permeated my nostrils and even as I licked and licked the lips of her cunt and nibbled her cherry-red clitty she was obviously in dire need of another fucking.

'Miranda's cunt was extraordinarily tight but I slipped my once-more rampant tool in without difficulty. The great girth of it, she exclaimed, felt most delightful and every stroke brought her nearer to the precipice of ecstasy. It was far larger than that of her gentleman admirer at home, she said; he being Mr Robert Coggins, the well-known musician who, they say, could even be the next Paganini, if only he were not so diffident.

'She arched her back to meet every lunge of my prick and I swear I have never penetrated a woman's cunt so deeply. I was up on my knees pumping into her, my hands cradling the firm white orbs of her bottom as she lay back on the pillows. Her titties had spilled out of her camisole and seemed to be dancing a jig of their own. All too soon my spunk gushed out into that wonderfully tight pussey but her loud moans and rolling eyes told me that her own pleasure had come upon her at the same time. Exhausted, I rolled off her and for a moment dropped off into slumber.

'We must only have been asleep for a minute or two when I heard a tap on the door and someone coming into the room.

'"Miranda? Are you awake?" came a woman's voice. "It's Angelica Thirkettle. I've brought you a preparation which I'm sure will help rid you of your head-ache."

'Oh my good God, I thought. I was well and truly caught, and could offer no valid excuse for my presence in Miranda's bed.

'"Captain Wilks!" exclaimed Mrs Thirkettle. "Why, this is an outrage! I am sure you have been taking advantage of Miranda here."

'"This isn't what it may appear," I managed to bluster.

'"Nonsense. I know perfectly well what is going

191

on. Get out of that bed this instant! My husband and I, in case you did not know, are great friends of Miranda's parents, and being their daughter's god-parents have promised to keep an eye on her for them. Is this the sort of behaviour they would expect? It is not, man! I am sure that my better half would like a word with you about this, and the sooner the better. He is at present in our chambers along the corridor. Get your clothes on and come with me."

'Angelica Thirkettle had a most authoritarian way of speaking. Though her voice was almost hushed, she had a way of commanding that which she sought in the most decisive manner. I had no option but to obey, and struggled into my shirt and trousers – I had no time to put on shoes and socks – before being bustled away to receive a dressing-down from Mr Thirkettle. As I stumbled along with Angelica close behind, I was reminded of a poor soldier being marched off to the guard-house.

'"In there, you vile man," cried Angelica, throwing the door wide. "I will be with you in a moment."

'I entered the room, which at first seemed deserted. Then, over at the desk by the window, I caught sight of Thirkettle's familiar bearded face, busy with some papers by lamplight.

'"Hello, Wilks," he said. "How are you? I'll be with you in a minute. Was that Angelica I heard just now?"

'His pen scratched away, and I stood there in my shirt feeling somewhat awkward and ill-at-ease. Not looking up for a moment from the task which absorbed him, Thirkettle hummed and whistled as he worked, and I found this deuced odd in view of the fact that his wife was behaving like some vengeful Valkyrie.

'"Nice day it's been, hasn't it?" he observed casually and then the silence returned, marked only by the ticking of an ormulu clock on the mantelpiece.

'At length he put down the papers he had been working on, and slowly replaced the top on his inkbottle.

'"I was talking to your friend Mr Feather about his work earlier," he said, unfolding a newspaper. "He's very good, isn't he? I think we might buy some of his pieces. He had a particularly good portrait of Miss Everleigh in the glen, which he had taken only very recently."

'I had scarcely opened my mouth to reply when an inner door in the Thirkettles' chambers crashed open and there to my surprise stood Angelica, dressed to my astonishment in the guise of a circus ring-master. She wore a top-hat and a long red coat, unbuttoned, which gaped open to reveal stays of shiny leather, over which her firm naked bosoms protruded, and drawers of a similar material. Save for long black riding boots and stockings, this was all she wore. In the one hand she carried a large hoop such as a child might chase down the street with a stick, and in the other a fearsome whip, which she brandished at me in a manner that quite made me tremble with fright.

'"Hello, my dear," said Thirkettle, glancing up from his paper. 'You haven't seen my cigar-case, have you? Ah, here it is. Care for a cigar, Wilks?"

'Angelica's appearance, and my situation, had rendered me temporarily speechless, and my mouth opened and closed like that of a goldfish in a bowl. In any case, the lady in question briskly answered his question for me.

"He won't be having a cigar, the vile seducer!" she growled. "By the time I've finished with him he'll never want to see a lady's bedroom again."

'She advanced on me, brandishing the whip in an alarming manner and forcing me to retreat further into the room.

'"Please, please," I cried. "There is a simple explanation to all this, I can assure you. Things are not quite as they might have seemed."

'"Rubbish!" she snarled, prodding me with the whip.

'"Look, I say, can't we be civilized about this? I mean, Miranda's a grown girl, and well able to look after herself, and indeed past her majority."

'"Is that Miranda you're talking about?" asked Thirkettle, from behind *The Times*. "Is she feeling better? She looked a bit poorly when I saw her before dinner. Funny, can't seem to find my matches."

'His wife ignored him, and drove me further into a corner.

'"Now then, you vile creature, I can see I am going to have to tame you." She cracked the whip so hard against the polished wooden floor it fair made me jump. "You will have to be taught some discipline."

'Then she came for me. I swear, though I have stood alone many times on the battlefields, I have never feared anything as much as I feared Angelica Thirkettle at that moment. I begged for mercy, but she would not be deterred.

"No, my man, we must teach you a lesson. You, as a military man, must know the value of self-control. If you act like an animal you must expect to be treated like an animal!"

'I had several times been forced to witness soldiers

194

undergoing a flogging, and it was not a pretty sight. I had no wish to be whipped like a cur, and yet I was completely intimidated by the *dominatrix*.

'She fixed me with an unwavering glare. "Now!" she exclaimed, cracking the whip again. "We saw you up to your tricks earlier, didn't we? Let's see you jump through this hoop!"

'She cracked the whip again, and again, and I crouched down on all fours, and before I knew what I was about I was springing through the hoop like a circus animal, just as she told me to. Down came the whip again, and once more I jumped. Every time that whip issued its fearsome crack I did what I was told, and never thought to query the ringmaster's authority.

'Finally, Angelica threw down the whip and hoop and burst into hoots of laughter. I was even more astonished than I was before, especially when I looked up and saw Miranda standing there as well, quite naked and quite beside herself with mirth. I realised now that I had been "had", and that it was all a jolly jape, and even old Thirkettle put down his paper and joined in the fun. The four of us then retired into an inner sanctum where we all fucked like fury for the next three hours. I had the double pleasure of fucking Angelica's arse whilst lapping at Miranda's open cunny that she placed directly onto my eager mouth.'

TO BE CONTINUED

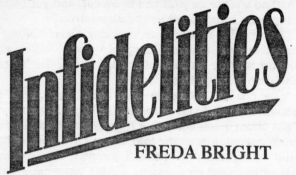

# Infidelities

## FREDA BRIGHT

The Petersens – the darlings of New York's most glamorous musical and medical circles. Seth, the golden boy of medicine, for whom the Nobel Prize lies within arm's reach. Annie, a woman with the power and determination to realise her potential both as a singer and supportive wife.

Why then, after 10 years of blissful marriage does Annie feel such an agonising, torturing doubt? There's no smear of lipstick, no stray earring, no furtive phonecalls – nothing to confirm her dread. But Annie knows for certain that their world is falling apart . . .

0 7221 1963 1    GENERAL FICTION    £3.99

# THE INTIMATE MEMOIR OF
# DAME JENNY EVERLEIGH

## BOOK ONE: THE EROTIC ADVENTURES OF A VICTORIAN LADY OF PLEASURE

Uncensored, unashamed Dame Jenny continues her erotic career amongst the cream of Victorian gentry. Her lusty narrative, as liberal as her appetite, as libidinous as her ample curves, is as joyous and unfettered as the forbidden fruits she so lovingly nurtures.

As she eloquently recalls her outrageous conquests, false modesty, she states, is foolish and vulgar. So take your seats, ladies and gentlemen, and hold fast, while Dame Jenny embarks on the adventure of a lifetime – a delicious and voluptuous journey of robust pleasure, endless arousal, enhanced by the sweet, stirring sensations of Jenny's pulsating prose!

And don't miss Books One, Two and Three in the sensational Memoirs of Dame Jenny Everleigh – also available in Sphere Books.

0 7474 0160 8    GENERAL FICTION    £2.75

A selection of bestsellers from SPHERE

## FICTION

| | | |
|---|---|---|
| WILDTRACK | Bernard Cornwell | £3.50 ☐ |
| THE FIREBRAND | Marion Zimmer Bradley | £3.99 ☐ |
| STARK | Ben Elton | £3.50 ☐ |
| LORDS OF THE AIR | Graham Masterton | £3.99 ☐ |
| THE PALACE | Paul Erdman | £3.50 ☐ |

## FILM AND TV TIE-IN

| | | |
|---|---|---|
| WILLOW | Wayland Drew | £2.99 ☐ |
| BUSTER | Colin Shindler | £2.99 ☐ |
| COMING TOGETHER | Alexandra Hine | £2.99 ☐ |
| RUN FOR YOUR LIFE | Stuart Collins | £2.99 ☐ |
| BLACK FOREST CLINIC | Peter Heim | £2.99 ☐ |

## NON-FICTION

| | | |
|---|---|---|
| CHAOS | James Gleick | £5.99 ☐ |
| THE SAFE TAN BOOK | Dr Anthony Harris | £2.99 ☐ |
| IN FOR A PENNY | Jonathan Mantle | £3.50 ☐ |
| DETOUR | Cheryl Crane | £3.99 ☐ |
| MARLON BRANDO | David Shipman | £3.50 ☐ |

*All Sphere books are available at your local bookshop or newsagent, or can be ordered direct from the publisher. Just tick the titles you want and fill in the form below.*

Name_____

Address_____

_____

Write to Sphere Books, Cash Sales Department, P.O. Box 11, Falmouth, Cornwall TR10 9EN

Please enclose a cheque or postal order to the value of the cover price plus:

UK: 60p for the first book, 25p for the second book and 15p for each additional book ordered to a maximum charge of £1.90.

OVERSEAS & EIRE: £1.25 for the first book, 75p for the second book and 28p for each subsequent title ordered.

BFPO: 60p for the first book, 25p for the second book plus 15p per copy for the next 7 books, thereafter 9p per book.

*Sphere Books reserve the right to show new retail prices on covers which may differ from those previously advertised in the text elsewhere, and to increase postal rates in accordance with the P.O.*